His Queen of Dar

Horror Stories Inspired by the Films of Val Lewton

by

Michael Samerdyke

Copyright © 2021 Michael Samerdyke

Also by Michael Samerdyke

Land Beneath the Shadows: Tales of Kurgania # 1

Lost Shadows: Tales of Kurgania # 2

Shadows of Forgotten Ancestors: Tales of Kurgania # 3

The Dragon Lover and Other Fantasy Stories

Invasion of the President Snatchers: Science Fiction Stories

Exit, Laughing Maniacally

The Dream Cabinet of Dr. Kino (Kino Trilogy # 1)

Featured Creatures (Kino Trilogy # 2)

The Curse of Dr. Kino (Kino Trilogy # 3)

Horror Cavalcade Vol. I (non-fiction)

Dedicated

to Sheldon Wigod

and the staff of the New Mayfield Repertory Cinema

the best place to discover the films of Val Lewton

Table of Contents

Introduction: Val Lewton, His Movies, and Me

Val Lewton (1904-1951) was born in Yalta in the Russian Empire as Vladimir Ivan Leventon. His family came to America when he was seven. As an adult, Lewton became a writer. Weird Tales, the magazine that discovered H. P. Lovecraft, Robert Bloch and Ray Bradbury, published Lewton's "The Bagheeta" in 1930, but Lewton tended to avoid the fantastic. His writing career (ten novels and six non-fiction books) eventually brought him to Hollywood, where Lewton worked as a story editor for David O. Selznick.

After Selznick restructured his organization in the early Forties, Lewton ended up at the troubled RKO studio, where he was put in charge of a production unit and told to make horror movies. Typically, the studio would give Lewton the title the marketing department believed had box-office potential, and Lewton would then have to come up with a story that "fit" the title.

Remarkably, Lewton was able to bring sophistication and depth to these films, which were quite popular during the Second World War and have enjoyed an enduring "cult" popularity since.

Lewton's horror films are frequently divided into two groups. The first group took place in the present and were set mainly in the United States. (They also, with the exception of The Ghost Ship, are focused on female characters.) These include:

Cat People (1942) directed by Jacques Tourneur

I Walked With a Zombie (1943) directed by Jacques Tourneur

The Leopard Man (1943) directed by Jacques Tourneur

The Seventh Victim (1943) directed by Mark Robson

The Ghost Ship (1943) directed by Mark Robson

Curse of the Cat People (1944) directed by Gunther von Fritsch and Robert Wise

The second group of horror was produced after Lewton had made two non-horror films. A management reshuffle at RKO brought in a new slate of studio bosses who insisted that Lewton return to the horror genre and brought Boris Karloff over to RKO to star in Lewton's return to the horror genre. The three films Lewton made with Karloff were set in Europe.

The Body Snatcher (1945) directed by Robert Wise

Isle of the Dead (1945) directed by Mark Robson

Bedlam (1946) directed by Mark Robson

Although the collaboration of Val Lewton and Boris Karloff started (at least from Lewton's perspective) as something of a shotgun marriage, the two swiftly came to admire each other. Karloff, who had been on the verge of becoming jaded about his career, once said that "Val Lewton saved my soul."

Lewton was planning to make a movie about Blackbeard the pirate with Karloff in the title role when RKO closed down his unit. Ostensibly, this was a promotion with an eye to enable Lewton to make big-budget films, but studio politics frustrated Lewton, whose post-Bedlam career consisted mostly of missed opportunities. He died of a heart attack in 1951.

Horror movie fans usually celebrate stars, such as Boris Karloff; directors, such as James Whale or Wes Craven; or writers, such as Curt Siodmak or Richard Matheson. By approaching his horror films in a serious spirit, Val Lewton became the rare, if not the only, producer of horror films to generate a fandom.

I had read about Lewton's movies before I saw them. One night in 1982, I went to the New Mayfield Repertory Cinema in Cleveland's Little Italy and saw a double feature of Cat People and I Walked With a Zombie. It was a truly magical evening. Between the movies, several people, all strangers, gathered in the back of the theater to talk about details in Cat People: the cat-like feet of the bathtub, the vividly-depicted cleaning woman, the discarded sketch of the panther, and the haunting "moya sestra" woman. We all felt an excitement about what we had just seen, quite a tribute to a film that had been made forty years earlier.

That night was the beginning of my interest in Lewton and his films. I have since seen all of his horror films. Cat People and The Body Snatcher vie to be my favorite. Each of Lewton's films has something to recommend it, and I have become adept at spotting Lewtonesque touches in other horror films as well

The twelve horror stories in this book owe their existence to Lewton's marvelous movies and their continuing hold on my imagination.

Zombies Walk Among Us

"Did <u>The Ranger</u> come out yet?" Frank asked.

He ran into the shadow of the Hall J. Kelley University belltower, where Pete and Greg leaned against the wrought-iron handrail. The two history majors exchanged a smirk as the last chimes of noon sounded.

Greg put on a serious expression as he turned to Frank.

"It's running late as always."

Pete chuckled.

"Admit it, Frank. You just can't wait to see your name in print again." He turned to Greg. "He does this every week. He grabs an issue of <u>The Ranger</u>, sees if they spelled his name correctly, and then complains when they cut the final paragraph from his review."

Frank raised his hands.

"You've got me dead to rights."

"What movie did you review this time?" Greg asked.

"<u>Zombies Walk Among Us</u>."

Pete snorted. "That is the film for the students here. They don't read anything. They can't write. All they want out of college is a Business degree and a job. Any movie deeper than <u>Porky's</u> loses them. All of which explains why Greg and I are your only readers."

The three started across the empty quad toward the snack bar. With each step, the sour expression on Frank's face deepened.

"Thanks a lot, Pete. It's good to know that all my writing efforts are futile."

"Is the movie any good?" Greg asked.

Frank brightened.

"For a low budget horror film, it does a good job. One or two of the cast don't know how to act, but it's a very clever film."

Greg gave Frank a puzzled look. "What exactly is the plot of the movie?" I've seen at least six different TV commercials for it, and I don't see how what they're showing could fit together into a coherent story."

"Six different commercials?" Frank stopped, amazed. "The ad campaign must cost more than the film."

Pete raised his hands to the skies. "I can't believe I know such people. How can you guys talk seriously about a junk movie? Any movie with the word 'zombie' in the title just isn't worth talking about."

Frank pointed at Pete.

"There speaks an open mind. Next thing you're going to say is that the only two filmmakers worth talking about are Bergman and Fellini because they're 'universal artists.'"

"Don't you dare put Eric Huntley's words in my mouth," Pete said.

"Or anything else of his," Greg said.

"That stuck-up sophomore whiz kid might be good for a laugh," Pete said, "but that's a real low blow."

"Okay, no more Huntleyisms."

The three continued on the way to the snack bar. Pete pointed at Frank.

"I'll hold you to that." They went up the stairs, and Pete pulled the door open. "Anyway, Frank, you've got to admit that trash is trash, even when an intelligent person writes about it, and horror movies are trash."

"Not if they're well done, they aren't."

Pete shook his head.

"Trash they are, and trash they shall remain."

Greg looked at Frank.

"So Zombies Walk Among Us is worth seeing?"

"Sure. If you liked The Howling, you'll like this one."

Greg shrugged. "I could see it tonight, I suppose."

"Hey, if you have the chance, see it."

Pete groaned. "I give up on you guys." He stepped out the line to the Snack Bar and raised his hand in a benediction. "Keep passing open windows, okay?"

"Keep passing open windows," Frank and Greg said.

XXX

Frank got to the room for Twentieth Century Europe a bit early and saw Greg sitting in his usual desk. This time, however, he looked irritated.

"Didn't you like Zombies last night?" Frank asked.

"I liked it." Greg gave Frank an odd look, as if he were trying to decide if he were dealing with a madman or something. "It was good, but it didn't have a lot to do with the movie you reviewed."

"What?"

"I mean, you really screwed up the plot in your review. Did you actually see the movie, or did someone tell you about it?"

"Hey, I always see the movies I review. I saw it Sunday afternoon and wrote my review that night."

Greg shook his head. "You made some big mistakes then. You said that the doctor from Haiti took the lead in fighting the zombies."

"Right."

"The zombies killed him in the first ten minutes of the movie."

"No way."

"They did."

"The plump black guy with a French accent? Always wore a white carnation?" Frank couldn't believe his ears.

"The same. He got off the plane from Haiti, went to his hotel room, and there was a zombie waiting for him. The zombie cut his head off."

Frank raised a finger.

"Just a minute. In the movie I saw, he went to the hotel room and found a skull on his bed. A tarantula came out of the skull, and he had to kill it."

The two looked at each other in silence. Frank couldn't believe he was having this conversation. If this were anyone but Greg telling him this, he'd insist it was a late April Fool's joke. But Greg never went in for jokes.

"Look," Frank said, "if the doctor gets killed at the start of the movie, who finally got rid of the zombies."

"The hooker." Greg didn't even have to think about his answer. "She had inherited some kind of voodoo power from her ancestors, and used it to get rid of the zombies."

"And that took place in the oilfield, right?"

"Right."

Frank sat there and didn't know what to think. Greg seemed too confident of his answers to be making this up on the spot. Actually, Frank had never known Greg to show much imagination before. Why should he lie about this movie now?

Sometimes, studios did make different endings for the same movie, Frank knew. The happy one would be for the US market, and the sad one would be for overseas. Still, it sounded like Zombies Walk Among Us had the same basic ending, the zombies getting destroyed in the oilfield, but two different heroes. Maybe this was part of a new marketing strategy. Every release print would be slightly different, so if anyone saw the movie in a different theater, it would be a different movie. That would make Zombies Walk Among Us the ultimate cult movie.

"Where did you see it?" he asked Greg.

"The Southgate."

That was where I saw it, Frank thought. So much for the different theaters theory. He shrugged. Still, he had seen it a few days before Greg did, so maybe they switched the prints around every night.

Dr. Bednak walked in and hung up a map of the Habsburg Empire. Frank sighed and opened a notebook. He had to go back and see Zombies Walk Among Us at the Southgate tonight.

XXX

He caught the last afternoon show. Sitting through the "Coming Attractions," Frank began to feel like Greg had pulled a great "April Fool's" on him. These were the same trailers that he had seen on Sunday. The movie itself opened as he remembered it. Credits rolled over a scene of zombies pushing up and out of the earth.

The zombies then lumbered on to kill a man whose car had broken down. Frank grit his teeth. He had been taken. This was exactly how the movie had started on Sunday.

"I'm going to tell Greg what a bastard he is," Frank said.

Then the movie cut to Atlanta, where a young newlywed couple grabbed their suitcases and told their parents they were off to Marston, the bride's family estate.

Frank felt his mouth open in astonishment. Who the hell were these blond, preppy people? They hadn't been in <u>Zombies Walk Among Us</u> when he had seen it before. They couldn't have been spliced in from another movie, since Marston was the name of the house that was the zombie center. But no one had lived there since the Civil War in the movie he had seen.

All smiles, the couple boarded the plane to New Orleans. Dumbfounded, Frank watched as a ticket snafu separated the lovebirds and put the husband, Jeff Horton, next to Dr. Blood, the French-accented, carnation-wearing hero.

"At least he's still in the movie," Frank said, settling back to relax.

By the time the plane landed in New Orleans, Jeff liked Dr. Blood so much, he offered to let him share the cab to the hotel. The movie gave a close-up of Dr. Blood, who seemed to look directly into the audience at Frank.

"Thank you, but no. I have other arrangements. But I feel that we shall meet again."

Jeff and Alicia, his bride, went off the hotel, while Dr. Blood got into a limo. The camera panned from Dr. Blood's face to the cobwebs over the ears of the zombie chauffeur.

"What the hell?" Frank asked.

This wasn't the movie he had seen Sunday, but it was just enough alike to be irritating. Just when he thought <u>Zombies Walk Among Us</u> was going in one direction, it shifted into something else entirely.

"At least Greg is as wrong as me," Frank said, watching the hooker, an important character in the version he had seen Sunday and the hero of Greg's version, get strangled by the zombie chauffeur.

Zombies Walk Among Us continued to unreel before Frank's disbelieving eyes. The Hortons arrived at Marston, a place coveted by the evil Dr. Blood. At night, the evil Haitian's music lured Jeff into the swamp – always a bad idea in any horror movie Frank had ever seen – and the hapless newlywed was transformed into a zombie.

"That's been done before," Frank said.

Dr. Blood sent the zombified Jeff after Alicia. After shedding a few tears, she blasted his head off with a shotgun.

"That's original," Frank said.

The shooting brought the police detective into the movie. Remembering him from Sunday's version, Frank sat up straighter. In Sunday's film, the detective and Dr. Blood had worked together against the zombie plague. This time, things went differently. The detective battled Dr. Blood, and the two of them fell into a quicksand pool.

"Never saw a movie swamp without one," Frank said.

Their leader gone, the zombies returned to the earth, but Frank sensed a difference in this ending. The zombies had not been defeated. They now simply lay dormant, waiting for the next time they could walk the earth.

The lights came up, and Frank saw that he was one of six people in the theater. None of his fellow moviegoers seemed as excited as he was. After all, they had just seen a routine horror movie and had no idea that it changed from screening to screening.

Frank walked out to the lobby, and the girl behind the counter waved at him. He recognized her as Sue, from last year's Psychology class, and he walked over.

"Hi, Frank, what's new?"

"Not much." He shrugged. "How are you doing?"

She laughed and indicated the empty lobby. "Busy."

"What's up with <u>Zombies Walk Among Us</u>?"

Sue frowned. "It's a stiff. That's why there's only two of us here now. Today, if you can believe it, is one of its busier days. At least people still want to see <u>Rocky III</u>."

"Anybody notice anything strange about the movie?" Frank asked. "Anyone complain about it?"

Sue shook her head.

"Have you ever seen it?" Frank asked.

"Are you kidding? I hate horror movies," Sue said.

"Has the distributing company switched prints on you guys? Is the print you showed today the one you showed yesterday?"

"Why shouldn't it be? There's no reason to change. They only do that when there's been an accident." She laughed. "Since the company that put that film out is so cheap, I doubt they'd send another print even then."

"Oh," Frank said.

"Why so curious? It's just a dumb movie."

"Somebody told me about it. They said they had seen it here, but what they told me about the plot doesn't match what I just saw."

Sue looked puzzled for a moment, but then brightened up.

"It sounds like that game where everybody sits in a circle, and the first person whispers a sentence to the person next to him, and that person whispers it to the person next to him, and on and on and when the sentence comes back to the first person, it's completely different."

"That must be it," said Frank, knowing that it wasn't. "Take it easy, Sue."

"Good-bye, Frank."

XXX

Frank noticed an evil smile on Pete's face when he approached him under the HJKU belltower.

"See this week's <u>Ranger</u>?" Pete asked.

"No."

"Somebody wrote a letter denouncing you."

Frank looked at Pete in disbelief. "For what?"

"For your review of <u>Zombies Walk Among Us</u>." Pete chuckled. "You apparently had no idea what the movie was about." He raised a finger. "Your crime, comrade, is confusing the subplot with the main plot. Come on, I'll let you read it in the snack bar."

When they selected a table, Pete gave Frank his copy of <u>The Ranger</u> and then went to get some pop.

"Dear Editor," the letter began. "If you want to improve the quality of your newspaper, you must begin by ending the services of Frank Javnik as film critic. His review of <u>Zombies Walk Among Us</u> was utterly incompetent. From his review, I formed the impression that the film concerned a homicide detective who tracks down a zombie cult.

"However, upon watching the movie, I realized that the detective was only a minor character, somewhat reminiscent of Arbogast (Martin Balsam) in <u>Psycho</u>, and the main plot of this film concerned the duel for supremacy in the zombie cult between two practitioners of black magic, Dr. Blood and Baron Voodoo, the latter a character to whom Mr. Javnik did not refer even once.

"It is obvious to me that a person who confuses the subplot for the main plot of a movie should not be your movie reviewer. Sincerely, Eric Huntley."

Frank blinked and tried to make sense of what he had read. He couldn't believe it. He could believe that Eric Huntley had written it, since Huntley was an asshole.

But who the hell was Baron Voodoo?

Pete came back holding a cup of Pepsi.

"That little bastard wants your job," he said. "He knows you're graduating. He's a sophomore, and he wants your job for next year." He took a sip of the pop. "Don't worry. Sally won't dump you because of this, and who cares who gets to be film critic next year? HJKU can fall off the edge of the earth after graduation for all I care." He took another sip. "Anyway, everybody who knows him knows that Huntley's the biggest asshole on campus."

Greg walked up, a copy of The Ranger in his hand.

"Next to Greg, of course," Pete said.

"Did you see Huntley's letter?" Greg asked.

"Just read it. Who the hell's Baron Voodoo?"

"Don't ask me! I'm just a jerk who saw the movie." Greg raised his hands in disbelief. "What's Huntley playing at, making up something like that."

"Oh for crying out loud." Pete stood up. "I can't believe you guys care about this crap horror movie." He picked up his cup. "Keep passing open windows, okay?"

XXX

Frank's fingers drummed on the steering wheel as he waited for the red light to change. He couldn't believe he was on his way to the Alcazar to see Zombies Walk Among Us for the third time.

"By now I'll have spent more than ten dollars on the stupid thing," he said, looking out the windshield at the iffy neighborhood he was driving through. The Alcazar, the last place in Taylorville still showing <u>Zombies Walk Among Us</u>, was somewhat close to HJKU and, more importantly, offered a Wednesday afternoon. The ad also promised "safe parking," a promise that disturbed as much as it reassured.

That old shopping center up ahead looked like the place for the Alcazar, he thought. The light turned green, and Frank stepped on the gas.

A blue Olds on the cross street shot into the intersection, as if neither the red light nor Frank's Skylark existed. Frank slammed on the brakes and thumped the steering wheel with his gut as the guy flew past his front bumper.

"Driving to the theater's scarier than the damn movie," Frank said when he finally got some spit back in his mouth.

He crossed the intersection, and turned into the shopping center parking lot. Signs on the lampposts declared that parking was for store customers only. Parking for the Alcazar was in the back of the theater.

Frank drove around to the back where he saw a parking lot surrounded by a wrought-iron fence. At the mouth of the lot was a small wooden guardhouse. As Frank pulled up, a black man in a green uniform came out and stood next to a long, striped, wooden arm that looked like it had been borrowed from Checkpoint Charlie.

"One dollar."

Frank fished out the money and then drove into the lot. After getting out of the car, he looked at the sharp iron spikes thrusting up to the clouds.

They would look better outside the Marston mansion than a theater, he thought.

"Good thing I didn't come to the night show."

"You gotta walk through that tunnel to get to the theater," the guard said and then retreated back into the guardhouse without seeing if Frank had paid attention or not.

"Thanks."

The tunnel had been part of a bank's drive-through window operation, but the bank had closed, leaving the window boarded up. Hamburger wrappers and cigarette butts lay here and there as Frank trudged through the tunnel. Once he reached the other end, he turned left and looked at the Alcazar.

A hint of that old, white-elephant, movie palace glamor still clung to the place. It must have been something back in the Twenties, Frank thought as he looked at the fluted columns that held up the sign. He walked to the center door, pulled it open, and stepped into a hallway of dirty mirrors. Dead center, between the doors and the ticket booth, stood a dry fountain, with Cupid standing on one foot to pour imaginary water out of a boot. As Frank walked by, he saw three pieces of gum stuck to Cupid's ass.

An older white man with thick glasses sat in the ticket booth and never looked in Frank's eyes, although he did sell him a ticket when Frank handed the money over. A tired, heavy set woman presided over the concession stand and smiled at Frank when she gave him his popcorn.

He had no trouble finding a seat in the auditorium. His fellow moviegoers numbered three, all graybeards. One snored, one read a newspaper, and one carried on a lively conversation with himself about Reagan. Frank took a seat on the aisle and studied the cobwebbed cherubs on the walls before the lights went out.

The movie started with the same old zombies-breaking-out-of-the-earth bit, so Frank paid attention to the credits themselves this time. None of the actors names meant anything to him, but the movie claimed to be based on a story by Herbert Travers.

That rang a bell. Frank leaned back and scratched his head. Hadn't Travers been one of the regular authors for <u>Weird Tales</u> after

Lovecraft died? It might be worth it to track down the original story, Frank thought.

The first scene, the stranded motorist getting killed by zombies, made Frank sit up and take notice. The motorist seemed younger than Frank remembered. It had to be a different actor. Frank thought this guy put up a much more vigorous fight than he remembered from the previous versions. Heck, this guy almost got into the woods on the other side of the road before the tall black figures finally broke the actor's neck.

The film cut to the newlyweds as they got on the airplane.

"We wouldn't have to hurry so much if you didn't take so long in the shower," Jeff said, giving his bride a bitter look.

"We're on time," Alicia said.

"Barely. It's been like this since I married you."

Frank blinked. They sure didn't sound like newlyweds anymore.

Alicia sniffed back some tears, and Jeff took her hand.

"Honey, I know it's been hard since the… miscarriage." He sighed. "Maybe now that we have Marston, it will be a second chance for us."

What was this? Frank turned to try to gage the reaction of his fellow moviegoers, but he couldn't make them out in the murk. A familiar voice rang out.

Dr. Blood was getting on the plane. His conversation ran like Jeff remembered. When the characters got to New Orleans, however, Jeff and Alicia rented a car to Marston, and Dr. Blood took a taxi to the hotel. No sooner did he enter his room, than he noticed a skull resting on the pillow on his bed.

"No way," Jeff said.

A spider emerged from the skull, and Dr. Blood crushed it, just like he had done the first time he had seen Zombies Walk Among Us. Frank blinked in astonishment.

The film now cut to the swamp around Marston. A tall, bald man floated across the dismal water on a coffin.

Frank relaxed a bit.

"Okay, they stole that from Son of Dracula." That kind of plagiarism was kind of reassuring now. Maybe this was just an average horror movie after all.

Jeff and Alicia came to Marston, under the eye of Baron Voodoo, who sent his zombies after them that very night. Jeff got his neck snapped faster than the motorist did, and the zombies tied up Alicia.

"Blood will tell," Baron Voodoo said. "You are descended from Madame Gruizot, and I will unleash her power within you."

Alicia then tried to twist her way loose while the Baron chanted his mumbo-jumbo. Alicia didn't get free of her ropes, but she nearly got free of her clothes, which Frank found more interesting. He watched her sweat and twist as her blouse ripped to reveal just a bit more of her bosom, and he realized he was getting stiff between his legs.

"Shit," he said, then looked away and exhaled deeply.

When he looked back, Alicia's skin had started to darken as the Baron continued to chant. From within Alicia, a different female voice began to chant with the Baron, as she shrank and became stout.

Frank's mouth opened, and his brow furrowed. How the heck could this movie afford effects like this? he wondered. He hadn't even seen anything like this in Raiders of the Lost Ark.

Alicia's skin reddened and turned a deep shade of brown, while her hair curled, and her lips and nostrils thickened. She was Madame Gruizot.

The rest of the movie sped by Frank as he tried to remember the transformation. Dr. Blood, a hapless good guy, arrived at Marston only to get a zombie's spear in the guts and die. Baron Voodoo's triumph didn't last long, however, since Madame Gruizot ordered the zombies to put him in a cauldron.

"Go forth, my children," she said once the Baron's screams had died away. "Track down and destroy all who enjoy our suffering, who watch us die and rise again for their pleasure. Find them and bring them to our special hell!"

There was no music over the end credits. Frank became aware of a deep snoring sound a few rows behind him. He leaped up and looked around, to make sure no zombies had gotten close to him while he was spellbound.

All he could see, as the house lights came up, was the snorer. The other two guys must have left already.

If the zombies hadn't gotten them first, Frank thought.

He tried to chuckle, but it got stuck in his dry throat. He left the snorer and the cobwebbed cherubs on the wall. He walked past the dry Cupid and the dirty mirrors, stopping to check his reflection to make sure he was alone.

I have to find that story by Herbert Travers, Frank thought. That might give me a clue to this mess.

XXX

HJKU's library didn't have any of Herbert Travers' fiction, but a book called <u>Fantasy Authors</u> said that Travers did most of his writing for <u>Weird Tales</u> and died when that magazine did, in 1954. "Zombies Walk Among Us" received mention as one of Travers' better stories, and the book said it had been anthologized often. Frank wrote down the titles and went out to catch the rapid for the Taylorville library downtown, Restoration Drama class be damned.

He looked up each of the four anthologies, but the library only had the last: The Undead Companion. His heart pounded as he went into the stacks, and he prayed that the book was here.

It was. Frank nearly wept. His hand shook as he reached for it, and, gently, he eased it off the shelf.

"Now I can solve this thing," he said.

He hurried to the check-out desk and rushed back to the rapid.

Halfway back to the campus, Frank couldn't wait any longer and started reading "Zombies Walk Among Us." The Forties setting and dialogue came as a shock. Blake, the hero, was a private eye, and Frank could practically hear Bogie's voice as he read the first-person narration. Apart from that, it seemed to Frank that Blake was pretty much like the police detective in the first version of the movie he had seen. Indeed, once Frank got used to the Forties atmosphere, he was right at home with the story.

Blake witnessed a strange murder and started to investigate it, aided by Dr. Blood, who had survived a strange encounter with a skull and spider in his hotel room. Zombies attacked Blake, but the sudden arrival of Kelly, a gangster's moll in Traver's original, but, Frank realized, the basis for the hooker in the early versions of the movie he saw, let him escape.

At this point, the rapid pulled into the campus stop. Frank cursed and shut the book, after noting that he had reached the middle of page 95. He then walked the four blocks back to the HJKU parking lot. He drove home and gave his mother very perfunctory answers to questions about his day. Finally, he got to his room.

Opening The Undead Companion to page 95, he began to read.

"Glass shattered in the front hallway as the zombie hordes pressed dumbly against the house. The unearthly beat of the voodoo tom-toms chilled Alicia's blood. Jeff struck at the grasping undead arms with a fireplace poker, but all his efforts seemed in vain."

Frank stopped reading.

What the hell was this? Alicia? Jeff? What happened to Blake, Kelly and Dr. Blood?

He flipped back to the beginning of the story. Blake and his tough guy narration were nowhere to be found. The story now opened with a letter both informing Alicia that she had inherited Marston and hinting at its ghastly past. Frank skimmed rapidly. Blake was the name of a dimwitted deputy sheriff, soon zombified. Dr. Blood perished by spider bite, and Baron Voodoo showed up as the leader of the zombies.

"No!"

Frank threw The Undead Companion across the room. This shouldn't be happening. Stories didn't change every time you read them.

The Undead Companion lay on the floor, daring Frank to try again.

He had to. He stood up and walked over to the book, his hands trembling. He bent down and somehow got hold of the book. His fingers flipped the pages to 95.

"Drums boomed in the night. Madame Gruizot stood on the verandah of Marston and regarded the mute army before her with pride as the torchlight danced on her ebony skin.

"They are coming, my children. Track them down and destroy all who enjoy our suffering!"

Frank screamed.

XXX

"Seen Frank today?" Pete asked Greg as they met under the HJKU belltower.

"No." Greg seemed baffled. "He missed Twentieth Century, and he knew we had a fifty-point quiz today."

"He was acting really odd the last week or so," Pete said.

Greg laughed. "How can you tell?"

Pete frowned. "No, seriously, you have to admit that he did seem nervous the last few days. He never misses class."

Greg shrugged. "I don't know. Maybe he just had some car trouble. He'll be back tomorrow."

Pete sighed and looked away. Then he shrugged.

"I guess you're right," he said. "Keep passing open windows."

XXX

Frank sped through the darkness, his headlights making a valiant attempt to cut the murk. Despite that, the darkness pressed ever closer against his car. Frank's throat burned for liquid, and his stomach had long ago tied itself into knots.

He had been driving ever since he had thrown The Undead Companion across the room that final time. He could barely remember stopping for gas, although he assumed he must have. He didn't even remember leaving the highway, but he was driving on gravel now. His mind couldn't focus on the details of his trip. All road signs glazed over when he looked at them. His eyes couldn't make out the mileage of the odometer.

He couldn't say where he was.

The Skylark reached a curve in the road and died. Frank sat behind the wheel for a minute but soon felt compelled to get out of the car, kick its tires, and curse.

Just like that idiot at the beginning of Zombies Walk Among Us, he thought.

Clumsy, cobwebbed feet advanced through the woods toward him.

A Ticket to the Night Zoo

Storm clouds loomed overhead as George stepped out of Fulton's. He squinted up at the sky. If it rained, he couldn't eat lunch in the zoo and would have to go to the Colonnade. By the time he walked to the zoo, ate, and walked back, he was sure to get wet. Going to the Colonnade would be the wise thing to do.

He glanced into Fulton's window and saw Mr. Fulton talking to a customer. George frowned. The day had been hellish. He deserved the zoo.

Hurrying along the sidewalk, he remembered the morning in all its ghastliness.

"What makes you type so late at night?" Mrs. B, his landlady, asked as he tried to leave for work. "People who work for real sleep nights. Maybe I kick you out at the end of the month."

The bus ride to Fulton's had been agony. Thanks to Mrs. B, he had missed the express and had to take a local. He ended up behind two blue collar types who competed in denouncing the new Taft-Hartley Act and that worm from Missouri who let Congress do such a thing.

Because he had taken a local, he arrived at Fulton's at 9:05 instead of 8:45.

"And how is our Hemingway this morning?" Mr. Fulton asked.

"I missed my usual bus. It won't happen again, Mr. Fulton."

"I expect my employees to be in their places when the doors open."

"Of course, Mr. Fulton," George said, regretting he had ever admitted starting to write a novel about Napoleon.

Just then a woman came up and asked if they had a copy of Forever Amber. Mr. Fulton retreated in disgust to his office to let George handle the sale.

The morning limped along after its miserable start, and then, fifteen minutes before lunch, Miss Higgins came in. George spotted her ridiculous green hat moving down the current affairs aisle and tried to flee, but the stout woman cornered him and, chins atremble, asked if he had read that new book about the atomic bomb.

"I'm afraid not."

"I think every thinking person should read it." Her blue eyes looked trapped behind the thick lenses of her glasses. "It actually made me feel sorry for the Japanese."

"Really."

"I could lend you my copy," she said. "More people have to become aware."

George was quite aware that Miss Higgins had set her green cap for him. At least once a week, she came into Fulton's to bother him about this book or that book, oblivious to the fact that he didn't care for her in the least. Now Mr. Fulton came out from his office to see to two customers who needed to be rung up.

"I don't pay you to play Romeo," he said. "If you can't keep your girlfriend out of this store, distracting you from the work I pay you to do, I'm going to have to let you go."

Miss Higgins blushed deeply and hurried out the door. One of the other customers snickered while George rang up the purchases. George wanted to kill the man on the spot.

Finally, finally, the chance came to leave Fulton's and go to lunch. He felt like an animal let out of a cage.

The zoo was two blocks from Fulton's. As he neared it, George realized that the threatening sky was keeping other people away. Hardly anyone dared the zoo under such ominous clouds.

The lemonade wagon's owner had started to pack up when George arrived. The man poured George a lemonade in bad grace, continually glancing up at the sky to see if the downpour would start.

The walkway past the elephants to the Cat Building lay empty before him. George hurried by the lumbering dumb beasts, scarcely giving them a look. The silence, the solitude of the deserted zoo embraced him. Mrs. B and Mr. Fulton, the loudmouths on the local, the earnestness of Miss Higgins, all died away. George walked alone to the Cat Building, enjoying the company.

The black steel-and-stone structure had always drawn him, ever since he started working at Fulton's. His first lunch in the zoo had been the day an old keeper died under the panther's claws. That afternoon, the old rummy's blood still lay on the floor of the outdoor cage when George had walked by, making his heart beat faster when he saw it. Reading about cities destroyed, even seeing it at the newsreels, had never reached that level of reality. That blood had been genuine. A man had died there.

The zoo hadn't replaced the panther yet. The outdoor cage sat empty, waiting a new tenant. George stared between the bars, remembering the rummy's blood, how dirty it seemed. Some do-gooders, alarmed by the old man's death, had started talking about tearing down the Cat Building and replacing it with a "zoo without bars" fantasy.

George hated the idea. The bars were the best part of the zoo. They let you know who was in and who was out. Simple and clear, unlike life.

The sound of a match striking pulled George back to the present. Tobacco smoke drifted past him, and he turned to see a tall woman with a cigarette.

She watched the cage as intently as he. A striking red hat sat atop her defiantly black hair. She exhaled twin streams of smoke and looked at him. George had never seen such striking eyebrows on a woman. Her eyes were the blue of a frozen lake, and he could not look away from them.

"I miss the panther," she said. "Don't you?"

Her voice held the trace of an accent. The short "i" in miss sounded like a long "e," and the "th" in panther came out as a "t." From other women, George would have found this distasteful. From her, however, it seemed natural, a part of her allure.

"I would have loved to have seen him," George said, "but I first came to the zoo just after... just after he killed that man."

She arched her eyebrows and took another puff on her cigarette.

"I too am new to Taylorville. I left New York because my sister died there."

"I'm sorry."

"The women of my family..." She looked away from George. "Are short-lived."

The first drops of rain splashed on the pavement. George looked up and got one in the face. The clouds boiled with the promise of immanent rain.

"Let's go inside," he said.

They hurried to the door of the Cat Building, reached the overhang, when she stopped and shuddered.

"I'd rather not go in," she said, as rain hit the ground behind her in sheets. "The smell."

"I understand." George nodded his agreement. The rank scent of the big cats made its way out here, but he didn't want to face the rain either.

"I hate getting wet," she said, watching the rain bounce off the pavement. She exhaled smoke. "I hate it."

"I've never cared for it either," George said. He became aware of his brown bag. "Would you like some lunch? I've got salami on rye."

Again her eyebrows arched.

"You will share food with me," she said in a tone that George couldn't tell was a question, statement or command.

"You have a lovely voice." He handed her half a sandwich. "I can't place the accent."

She laughed and explained about the accent. George had become somewhat expert on European geography while following the war news, but he still couldn't place what she said. Maybe she was talking about provinces instead of countries, he decided.

She had always liked zoos, she continued to say, the big cats in particular. The family crest and all that. Best of all, she liked the night zoo. Everything seemed freer there. The beasts were more powerful. Dangerous. That was glorious.

It didn't make sense to George. In fact, it sounded like pure hooey. But as he listened to her say it, wrapped around her accent, it almost seemed as if the night zoo existed. As if it were a place as real as the Taylorville Zoo.

By now the rain had stopped except for a few drops falling from the overhang. Blue skies broke through the weakened clouds overhead.

"I have talked too much," she said, turning to George and kissing him.

The kiss tasted warm and bitter. As she turned away, George felt excited. He didn't meet beautiful women who kissed him every day. He blinked, and she was already far from the Cat Building, walking away fast.

He raised his hand to call and wave to her, but his watch caught his eye.

It couldn't be that late, could it? Twenty minutes past one?

The clouds had started to darken again when George got back to the shop.

Mr. Fulton purpled as he saw him.

"Where were you? Do you know what time it is?" He took three deep breaths. "June is on her lunch break, and I've had to handle things by myself."

George barely paid attention. His mouth still tingled from the kiss. Mr. Fulton would never understand.

Already, though, the memory of that glorious moment had started to fade. What color was her hat? Her dress?

What was her name?

She had never said.

George froze. She had never said. Three million people lived in Taylorville, and he loved a woman he knew nothing about. Without a name, he couldn't even find out where she lived, couldn't call her up, couldn't see her again.

"I'm trying to run a business." Mr. Fulton stepped right in front of George's face. "Are you listening to me?"

George looked around the store. Empty. The erratic weather kept the people away. He had lost the only woman he had ever loved, the only woman who understood him, and this jerk was worried about non-existent customers.

"Just shut up!"

Mr. Fulton blinked, and George punched him in the mouth.

The old man looked stunned as he went down on his keister. Blood welled up on his lip. George's hand tingled with excitement where he had hit Mr. Fulton. Laughing, George grabbed a pile of Faulkner and threw the books against Fulton's chest.

"You're crazy!"

The old man's body reeked of fear. George smelled it coming off him like yellow fog. He laughed because the man who had ruled his life for three years feared him. He actually feared George.

George laughed again, pulling his lips back, baring his teeth. From below, Mr. Fulton squirmed some more, and George's laugh turned into a snarl. His tongue briefly protruded from between his teeth.

The old man turned over and started to rise. George put his hands together and clouted Fulton in the shoulders. The old man went down and caught his forehead on the edge of a table. His skin ripped and blood flowed.

George screamed at the sight and fell on Mr. Fulton. He thrust his fingernails into the old man's neck and watched the blood course out.

"George." Mr. Fulton tried to pull away.

George dug deeper, maddened by the blood, maddened by the fear. He could taste it. Those who feared had to die. He held onto the struggling old man until he could smell the death smell rise to him.

He had smelled it before. When he had stood outside the panther's cage at the zoo, that day with the blood still on the floor. He hadn't known it was the death smell then, he hadn't known how to read the smell, but he knew it now.

He wiped his hands on Mr. Fulton's clothes, then stood up and walked to the window. Rain was striking the pavement again. Sunset wouldn't be for another five hours, he knew. He didn't want to wait around with the corpse. June was due back.

He put on his overcoat and stepped outside.

He hurried to the bus stop, hating each raindrop that landed on him. He stood by the round metal sign, sensing the little puffs of fear from the other passengers. He ignored them.

The express came soon enough. The door squealed open, and he hurried up the steps and dumped a handful of change into the box.

"Hey, that's too much!" the driver said.

He had always walked back to a window seat behind the rear wheels, annoyed at the man. People always dropped coins into the box. He had dropped coins into the box. He would soon be finished with buses anyway.

No one sat near him as the express rolled along the wet streets. A few men made their way back toward the empty seats around him, but after glancing at him, they ended up holding the bar as they stood in the front half of the bus.

When the express came to his stop, he bolted out of his seat, ran the length of the bus, and dashed down the steps into the rain. The freedom from the stale human smells on the bus pleased him, and he shrugged and stretched his arms. The overcoat and shirt felt too confining, and he shed the coat at the first trash can he passed.

He stood before his apartment house door. He pulled at it and walked in from the rain. the dark narrow stairway reminded him of the panther's cage, and he relaxed. He took the stairs three at a time, not caring if any saw him. Soon enough, he stood before his own door. Like the other door, he pulled at it.

Nothing happened.

There had been some ritual, he remembered. He reached into his pocket and touched something metal. Brow furrowed, he pulled it out and looked at it. It didn't feel right in his hand, too puny and fragile.

Yet something told him he had what he needed. He jammed it into the door and, following the commands of memory, turned it.

He pushed, and the door opened. Growling, he walked inside and slammed the door behind him.

The typewriter and some paper sat before him on a little metal stand. The sight of it hurt him, and he upended the stand. The typewriter hit the floor with a satisfying crash.

His shoes felt impossible now, so he kicked them off and tore the socks from his feet. His constricting shirt came off next, and he flung himself on the sofa, trying to think about how much time remained until sunset.

He looked up at the waning daylight on the opposite wall and forgot about everything else until the door opened.

"Mr. Walker, you left your key in the door," Mrs. B said. "That isn't safe."

He leaped off the sofa with a snarl, knocking her to the floor as she screamed. He growled and struck at her flabby white throat with his teeth. Her blood tasted hot and good. She struck at him, but her blows soon weakened. He held onto her aged flesh with his teeth until her spasms stopped.

Shouts came up the stairs, through the open door. He released the body and ran on all fours out the door and down the stairs. The odor of fear and the slamming of doors met him. A metallic clicking sound behind him signaled danger, so he jumped through the window over the landing, a heartbeat before an explosion roared behind him and something whizzed past his shoulder. He fell to the ground, landed on his front feet, rolled, and jumped over the short wrought iron fence.

He loped along the wet sidewalk. Too soon, too soon, he thought. Nightfall was so far away. He ran to the zoo, the only sanctuary he knew.

Thunder crashed, and rain bucketed down. He turned a corner and surprised a man with a bloody apron who threw a huge metal can at him. The can hit his shoulder, and every step from then on gave him pain. He slowed and tried to favor his other side.

Between the thunderclaps, a new sound arose. Piercing wails began to draw near. He remembered they meant danger. He stopped and sniffed the air, wondering what to do. He remembered the smell of tobacco, the sound of a match, and a bitter kiss. He continued toward the zoo.

When he saw the big gray-and-black gates, he forgot the pain in his shoulder and ran furiously. A black-and-white car screeched into his field of vision, and something exploded. Force struck his body and turned him, so he faced the car. Two men stuck their heads out as he turned back to the zoo gate.

He limped beneath it when he heard a second explosion and felt more agony.

He landed on the pavement and bled. So much time until night, he wept, as the rain poured over him.

His ears twitched as he heard several pairs of feet splashing toward him. He growled and pushed himself forward.

Explosions came all the time now, and more pain, as he thrust toward the cage. He roared, and blood streamed from his mouth until he fell down, letting his life run down the sidewalk. Darkness came suddenly.

Darkness surrounded him as the men came up to point at his corpse and chatter over his wounds. Their noise meant nothing to him.

"Come," she called, and he heaved himself up, past his corpse, past the chatterers. He walked without pain, and he twitched his tail with delight.

"Come." Her voice was a command, and he obeyed, running to the night zoo, where his mistress waited.

She opened a door for him, and he entered the big outdoor cage. Blood covered the floor. He lapped at it and looked out through the bars at the night sky.

She closed the cage behind him. The noise made him look back. When he turned forward, he could see a crowd of chatterers standing on the other side of the bars. Their pale dead faces looked at him with terror. They reeked of overpowering fear.

He lowered his head and lapped the blood again, then began to pace the length of his cage. He had come home.

My Sister

I never expected to meet anyone like Sonya.

I almost didn't go to the Sons of Caligari meeting that night. It was a snowy January evening in Taylorville, and the driving would be painful. I had been typing mailing lists all day, and I just wanted to change my life. Spending yet another Friday evening talking about horror movies with old friends didn't see like a way out of my rut.

And then I met Sonya.

XXX

"Texture."

That's what Ralph was saying when I walked in.

I groaned. Ralph had probably gotten a job selling carpet or something. He changed jobs a lot, and no one can go into the details of a job you don't care about more than Ralph.

"What do you think, Pete?" Ralph asked. "Al says that what makes a movie great is its texture."

I relaxed. If texture was Al's idea, we could kick the topic around for a few hours.

"You mean how a movie feels between your fingers?" I winked at Al.

Carole, Joe's wife, thumped me on the shoulder and took my coat. The Belchaks were hosting the Sons of Caligari this month. I had it next month, although my landlady, Mrs. Dobrush, always eyed me funny for days afterwards. I hated hosting the winter meetings. In summer, I'd always suggest going to the park for a cookout.

The Sons of Caligari, the baleful offspring of the <u>Creature Feature</u>, was formed on the playground of St. Mark's Elementary from the union of some crazy Kurganian-American kids and the exasperation of Mr. Murzentik, our principal. "You kids are always talking about horror movies. Why don't you do something about it?" he asked.

We ended up inflicting a live performance of <u>House of Frankenstein</u> on an unbelieving Eighth Grade, and they inflicted a ton of grief on us. That sealed our friendship. Me, Ralph, Al, Tony, Joe and Carole have been talking horror movies ever since, which probably wasn't the outcome Mr. Murzentik had wanted.

"The Art Museum's going to show <u>Nosferatu</u> next month," Al told me as I helped myself to the potato chips. "With live organ music."

"That'll be different." I crunched a chip. "Maybe we can meet for pizza and drive over to see it, and that can be our February meeting."

"No." Al stuck his hand into the pretzel bowl. "I don't want to miss seeing your landlady glare at us." He gave me a look of mock disapproval then laughed. "Maybe we should teach her the <u>Wolf Man</u> poem. She could be the next Maria Ouspenskaya."

"There'll never be another Ouspenskaya," I said. "She's an immortal of the screen."

The telephone rang, and I watched Carole answer it. It must be nice to be married, I thought. It must be nice to get phone calls.

I turned to look out the window at the snow. Joe and Carole lived on a side street that got plowed only when the crews felt good and ready, and the snow-filled tire tracks put me in mind of how the Carpathian mountain passes must have looked in winter, when a young Bela Lugosi defended the Habsburg Empire against the Romanovs.

Joe offered me a 7-Up.

"Heard about your story yet?" he asked.

"They rejected it. 'Too traditional.' 'Couldn't connect.'" I shrugged. "The usual slop."

"Maybe you should send it to <u>Fantastic</u>. That editor liked your stuff."

"But never enough to buy it," I said. "Besides, they fired him. This rejection was from <u>Fantastic</u>."

"Everybody sit down!"

Carole, a huge smile on her face, stood in the center of the living room.

I looked at Joe, who shrugged and sat. I sat down too.

"That was Tony." Carole gave Al, Ralph, and me a look that could only be described as significant. "And he's bringing a date."

We could hear the snow fall outside.

"Wow," Ralph finally said.

"Does he know what he's doing?" Al asked. "I mean, if she meets us, she'll never go out with him again."

I laughed. "Maybe that's his plan."

"Well, I'm glad he's bringing a date," Carole said. "At least there'll be one other sensible person here."

About fifteen minutes later, Tony's car pulled up. Ralph looked like he wanted to go to the window to spy on them, but Joe shook his head, so Ralph just took more pretzels instead.

There was a knock at the door. Carole opened it, and Tony walked in, followed by a tall woman with sharp black eyebrows. She took off her white beret, and I could see the gorgeousness of her raven-colored hair that streamed to the shoulders. As she unbuttoned her coat, I felt angry that Tony had seen and won her first.

"Hello," she said, a trace of uncertainty underlining the word.

"Hi," I said.

Al stood up and spread his arms, as if to take us all in as he never took his eyes off Tony's date. "Tony, introduce us, please."

Tony beamed. "Sons of Caligari, meet Sonya Durzek. Sonya, these fiendish characters are the Sons of Caligari. From the TV set left we have Al, Ralph, Pete, Joe and Carole. Carole isn't technically a Son, but once she married Joe, we were stuck with both her and the old name of our club."

Sonya nodded. "I am pleased. Tony has told me so much about you. You all went to school together and made a play about Frankenstein."

A groan burst out of me, and I looked at the floor. "Tony! How could you tell her something like that?" I remembered standing before my uncomprehending classmates with an old wig taped over my face. I made myself look at Sonya. "I played the Wolf Man. The peak of my acting career."

Sonya gave me the ghost of smile before Al, who just looked pained, began explaining.

"I was never so embarrassed. Everyone who liked horror movies was in the play, and the students in the audience didn't know what we were doing. They looked at us like we were singing in Martian. I was so glad when Ralph dragged me into the closet."

"The closet?" Sonya asked, and I decided I loved the way her eyebrows arched.

"What we used for a quicksand swamp," I told her. "We had a lot less of a budget than even a B movie."

"Ah," she said, and I could see understanding dawn in her eyes.

"But we survived," Al said, and he held the potato chip bowl out to her. "Tell us about yourself. How did you meet Tony?"

"Isn't she great?" Tony put his arm around her shoulder and kissed her. "I met her when I took Aunt Vika to the Kurganian Women's Hall. They were showing some interwar operetta…"

"Apple Blossoms," Sonya said.

"And there was Sonya, like a rose between those old thorns."

You couldn't pay me to go to those interwar operettas. Granny had dragged me to enough of them way back when. I had even seen Apple Blossoms a couple of times. Yet, I realized if I had gone once more, I would have met Sonya first.

"I introduced myself to her," Tony said, "and it turns out that Sonya's new in Taylorville. She's actually from Kurgania, but her folks left it when she was a kid. Back in the Sixties, was it?" he asked. Sonya nodded. "She's lived in Chicago most of her time here, though."

"Have you gone back since '89?" Carole asked.

"Twice," she said. "It's much better now. I feel more comfortable there. I am going back to Radlova in a month."

"She's not from Radlova," Tony said quickly. "Her people are from a small town in the southeast."

That cheered me up. Grandpa had come from east of Sorgava, and he taught me that the Radlovans were all jerks.

"But please—" Sonya raised her hands. Her fingers were so long and elegant that I nearly gasped. "Don't talk about me. Tony has told me so much about your conversations. Please do what you usually do. I would be very interested."

Everybody stood in silence, not wanting to go first. What if she found us silly too?

Finally I said: "Al was talking about texture."

Tony took a step back.

"Texture?" he asked.

"That's how a movie feels between your fingers," I said.

Joe threw a pretzel at me. Al looked like he wanted to throw something heavier.

"Texture," he said to Sonya as he stepped forward so his back was to me, "is the feeling a movie gives that there is a reality beyond the story itself. The sense that there's a bigger world than what we were watching for 90 minutes. Texture gives you a feeling that the world you are watching contains more than just one story."

"Explain, professor, for us dunces," Joe asked.

Al rubbed his hands together.

"Whenever you have minor characters who are more than just stick figures who exist to be bumped off by the monster, you have texture. Those characters point at a life that is not on the screen, at stories the camera chooses not to follow."

"So what does that have to do with horror movies?" Ralph asked, before he bit into a potato chip.

"Exactly! Our challenge is to think up examples of texture from horror movies and then come up with stories to make into new movies."

That was a good challenge. I sat down and thought. There were hints of bad blood between the Burgomeister and the Una O'Connor character in Bride of Frankenstein, but I didn't think that could carry a story, to say nothing of a whole movie.

Sonya walked over to get a can of pop off the table, and inspiration struck as I watched her move.

"Cat People," I said. "That scene in the restaurant, where that woman comes up to Irena and says, 'My sister.' She's gone from the movie after that, but we know she must be cursed like Irena herself. What happened to her could make a good movie."

Al smiled. "I was hoping somebody would come up with that."

Carole rolled her eyes. "Trust Al to stick up for Val Lewton."

"Which movie is this?" Sonya asked.

Al went into his encyclopedic mode. "Cat People, 1942, RKO, directed by Jacques Tourneur, produced by Val Lewton, starring Simone Simon. She plays Irena, a Serbian immigrant. She falls in love with Oliver, although she believes that she is cursed to become a cat if she marries. They marry, but she, ah, she, uh…"

"Remains aloof," I said.

"Thanks, Pete," he said, and gave me a look that told me I had been forgiven. "She remains aloof from her husband. Oliver has her seen Dr. Judd, a shrink, but Oliver also finds himself attracted to Alice, a co-worker, who gets followed by a big cat at night. Dr. Judd tries to force himself on Irena, and she turns into a big cat and kills him but is fatally wounded."

Sonya took a sip of her drink. "Interesting."

Carole applauded. "Good job, Al. You kept it under five minutes. Usually, Sonya, that movie can make him go on for hours."

Al blew a raspberry at Carole and turned back to Sonya.

"Now when Irena and Oliver get married, they meet an eerie cat-like woman who looks at Irena and says—"

"*Moya sestra*," Sonya said.

"Great pronunciation. We never see her again in the movie. She is only there to cast a shadow on Irena's wedding day, but she gives Cat People texture."

I interrupted Al. "I see where you're going. If she's one of the cat people like Irena, then what happens to her?"

"Hey, that's what they should have built the sequel around," Ralph said. "Then it could have been really scary."

"That's our challenge for tonight," Al said. "Let's figure out a real sequel to Cat People based on the '*moya sestra*' woman."

I was excited. This had potential. Cat People's real sequel was a good movie, but it wasn't really a horror film. RKO forced Lewton to make a movie called Curse of the Cat People, and in revenge he made a movie without cat people. For myself, any movie about a lonely child with an imaginary playmate hit too close to home to be comfortable viewing, and I just couldn't enjoy Curse of the Cat People as much as the original.

"I think this woman would have left New York."

All of us looked at Sonya. None of us expected her to play the game. Had she even seen Cat People?

"After all," she said, "if someone as prominent as Dr. Judd, a nationally-known psychiatrist, had been killed, it would have been in all the papers. Her instinct for self-preservation would have made her leave the city."

"But I thought you never saw the movie?" Joe asked.

"I have. Not in America, but in Europe. They retitle movies for different countries, you know. Cat People meant nothing to me, but once Al started describing it, I remembered Her Lips Destroy, which I saw over there."

"Her Lips Destroy," I said, trying it out. "It certainly fits the movie."

"Leaving New York would make sense." Al was eager to build this movie that would exist only in his mind. "Where does she go? Los Angeles?"

Ralph laughed. "She could go to Hollywood and meet Abbott and Costello."

We groaned, and Carole stuck a sofa pillow over his mouth.

Sonya paced around the room as if she hadn't even noticed Ralph. "Los Angeles is too far and too foreign. She wants her people around her, wants to hear the old language. Remember, she cannot speak English very well."

"We ought to give her a name," I said. "She can't be just 'she' for the whole movie."

"Danica then," Sonya said. "Danica leaves New York for the Midwest, for a city like Taylorville or Chicago, and she gets a job in a restaurant."

Ralph, recently liberated from Carole's pillow, smirked. "Everybody's gotta eat."

Sonya's eyes glared for a moment. "She doesn't work with the food. She provides atmosphere. She sings or plays an instrument to give bored Americans or homesick immigrants the illusion of being some other place in a happier time."

"That all makes sense," Al said, "but what about conflict? This is supposed to be a horror movie."

"Conflict." Sonya paused and regarded her reflection in the window. "Conflict always comes to such beings. A man is attracted to her. A harsh man, a policeman. Victor. He senses the danger that surrounds her and is intrigued. Danica, meanwhile, finds herself attracted to another man, one as alone as herself."

She turned to look at Tony, and one of Carole's candles guttered for a moment. None of us would have dreamed of interrupting her. Sonya sighed and continued the imaginary movie.

"This man, Robert, is a poet, and every night he comes to the Old Sorgava to write verse, drink, watch Danica perform, and imagine himself rubbing shoulders with the great Romantic poets.

His poetry, while heartfelt, is not the current thing." She shrugged. "He would be happier in an earlier time."

Sonya leaned forward, spread out her fingers, and sank them into the swivel chair's back, as if it were an enemy's neck.

"Victor, of course, is no fool. He knows Danica loves the poet. He thinks a beating will send his rival away, and one night, after Danica's performance, he gets Robert into an alley behind the Old Sorgava and beats him. Savagely."

She paused and closed her eyes, as if remembering an old wrong. I wanted her to open her eyes and continue with the story. It must be an old storyteller's trick, I thought, but it worked. Sonya had me believing that she really knew these people.

"Danica sees this, of course. She was standing in the stage door when the fight started. The beating unleashes her curse. She runs into the night and transforms. She hunts and kills one of the regulars at the restaurant, a rather pompous old man."

Her fingers dug deeper into the chair, and we all sat quietly and listened to her breathing.

"Naturally, Victor is assigned to this murder case. His presence around the Old Sorgava keeps Danica tense, keeps her transforming into a beast."

Sonya released the swivel chair and looked at her fingers, as if astonished at what she had been doing to the innocent chair.

"One night, Danica attacks another Old Sorgava fixture, the head waiter. He had always believed that he could have his way with her. He was a fool. Unfortunately, his death cries attract Victor and the police, and Danica, as a beast, is shot but escapes."

Sonya now stood center-stage in the room, her eyes fixed on a blank spot on the wall over the sofa as if she were watching these bygone events unfold and was telling us about them because we were all too blind to see.

"Robert finds her in human form, sees the wound, and guesses her true nature and guilt. Nevertheless, he takes her to his apartment. Victor, following the blood, arrives to take Danica away. Victor despises Robert and is careless. Robert gets Victor's gun and kills him. Their struggle, however, changes Danica back into a wounded beast. She kills Robert, her champion, and flees into the darkness."

Sonya closed her eyes. I became aware of the kitchen clock ticking as I waited for her to finish her movie, but then I realized that she would say no more. I blinked and looked at Al, who was also coming out of Sonya's spell. We looked at each other with the same thought. Sonya, this beautiful woman, had just come in and beaten us, the Sons of Caligari, at our own game. Tony would have to bring her back another night. He just had to.

I glanced at Tony, whose face glowed with adoration for this beautiful, imaginative, passionate woman he had found. The work jealous couldn't even begin to describe my feelings.

"It doesn't work," Ralph said. "Danica has to be Serbian. She wouldn't be at a restaurant called the Old Sorgava. Also, she can't escape at the end. She has to die at the end of the movie. That's how censorship worked back then."

Sonya made a little bow. "I had forgotten she was Serbian, but that is easily fixed. She works at the Old Belgrade then. As to the ending, I think I wanted to leave things open for a sequel, as Danica would escape and have Robert's child and the curse continue to another generation. But, yes, the censorship. It would be better if Danica died."

"No, you were great," I said as I stood up. "I mean, you did a great job. You described the story so well; I could see it in black-and-white. Danica was already wounded, right? The fight with Robert makes her bleed more. She gets out of the apartment and heads toward the river. She has to stop by these railroad tracks, and she dies as the sun rises."

Sonya fixed me with a warm smile.

"Thank you, Peter. You got me out of my difficulty."

She then looked at Tony and moved her left arm, so her wristwatch glittered. He looked at his watch.

"Oh, wow, we'd better get going. Carole, Joe, thanks for letting me bring Sonya."

"We wouldn't have missed it for anything," Carole said.

"It was a pleasure." Sonya put her coat on. "I hope to come to another one."

"We'd love to have you," Al said.

"Next month is at my place," I said as Tony opened the door.

"I hope to come, but who knows what lies ahead?" Sonya gripped Tony's hand. "I may have to go back to Kurgania sooner than I think."

"Well, we'll all be in Taylorville," Ralph said. "We don't get around much."

"No, you don't," Sonya said. "Good night." She and Tony waved goodbye and walked out into the snow.

"It ain't a fit night out for man nor beast," Joe said in his best W. C. Fields' voice as he shut the door behind them.

XXX

I couldn't sleep that night. Every time I shut my eyes, I could see Sonya, or was it Danica?, in the Belchaks' living room in black-and-white. I told myself it didn't matter. I couldn't have the real one or the imaginary one.

I quit trying to sleep and wrote out in longhand what I remembered of Sonya's tale. Maybe I could make something out of it. And after I wrote it, <u>Fantastic</u> could tell me how the story was too traditional, and <u>F&SF</u> could send me a smooth note about how it "did not meet our needs" that would leave me wondering if anyone had looked at it. After that, nobody else would read the story.

I kept writing anyway. Danica's story would keep me linked to Sonya. It would be a collaboration between us. Tony could have her body, and I would have this unpublishable story.

As I wrote down my ideas for Danica's death scene, I remembered why I'd had her die by the railroad tracks. Two blocks from Mrs. Drobush's house was Harrison Park, and if you jumped the fence behind the first picnic area and ran down the hill, you would come to five railroad tracks that stretched to downtown Taylorville. It was the most desolate spot I knew. Ever since the Sixth Grade class picnic, when I struck out with my bat on my shoulder and climbed over that fence to get away from everybody's laughter and stood there looking down, those metal tracks made me think of death, stretching into the city and also into the countryside, ignored by everyone else, but still lying there in wait.

I dressed and walked out into the snowy morning. The steam from my mouth chugged past my head as I hurried down to Harrison Park. The snow gave everything a clean look, and I tried to ignore the cold.

As I reached the picnic area, I noticed that someone else already stood by the fence. I thought I recognized the long black hair and white beret, and I doubled my effort at marching through the snow.

"Sonya!"

She didn't look at me. Her gloved hands gripped the chain link fence, and she looked down at the tracks. I reached her and caught my breath as a southbound diesel pulled its way through the snow on its way out of Taylorville.

"Is this where you thought Danica would die?" she asked as she watched the train. "It wasn't like this at all."

"Tony?" I asked.

"He's fine. He'll be fine." She turned to me. "He'll live to be a grandfather."

I must have looked puzzled because she laughed at me and turned away.

"Why did you come here?" I asked.

"My k… I am drawn to lonesome places and the people I find there."

"Your movie last night." I tried to figure out what to say. "It was so real, but it didn't even exist."

Sonya looked into the distance, away from Taylorville. "It was real. All of them lived." She shrugged. "And died."

"The curse was passed on to another generation?"

Sonya left the fence and started walking back to the road. I hurried after her.

"Look, next month, we're going to go to the Art Museum and see Nosferatu. With live organ music."

Her lips stirred in a sort-of smile.

"I'd like you to stay in Taylorville," I said.

"I must go back to Kurgania," she said. She threw her head back and laughed. "To see the spring thaw swell the Kolada once more and smell the apple blossoms."

My face got red.

"This isn't some damn operetta."

She stopped and looked at me. "No, it isn't. And it isn't a horror movie either for you and your friends to discuss and act out with wigs pasted on your faces. When the dead die, they stay dead, and the killers wash the blood off their hands and don't forget the screams."

Her features were tight with anger, and I could imagine her eyes in the face of a great cat in the moment before it leaps and kills. I couldn't say anything.

"Go back to your friends. They're nice. You're nice. Enjoy Murnau's film and the one after that."

Sonya turned and strode through the snow, out of the park. As she passed the gate and veered left, I suddenly started to run. I shook as I ran, and my throat dried up, but my feet plunged through the snow, and I closed in on her.

"Sonya!"

My voice sounded like a croak, but she looked back, surprised. I took her hands and gripped them.

"I want to go with you. To Chicago or Kurgania. Even to Hell. I want to go with you no matter what."

I leaned forward and kissed her. Her lips felt hot. I remembered that other title she mentioned. Her Lips Destroy. I didn't pull away.

Sonya put a hand to my cheek and broke the kiss. Her fingers slid over my lips.

"You know that those who love my kind die," she said.

"I know that," I said, looking into her pale brown, nearly yellow, eyes. "But I also know that they are loved."

Her lips smiled, but the warmth failed to reach her eyes, which remained focused on some black-and-white scene I would never be able to see.

"Come then," she said. "We'll help each other pack."

XXX

When I looked in those eyes, I nearly felt like running.

But run back to what? Mrs. Drobush's house? A pile of rejection slips?

So, Al, you inherit my stories. You can use them to start the next Sons of Caligari cookout or keep them in a shoebox until you decide to throw them out. They don't matter anymore.

And if you read sometime about an unidentified body that sounds like mine being found near railroad tracks in Chicago or New York or even Sorgava or Radlova, don't make a big thing about it. I won't be the first one, or the last one. But I'll probably be the only one who went into it knowing the odds and not caring about what happened before the final fadeout.

As long as I loved Sonya.

Shadows and Torment

"As we look objectively at the body of Mike Vlasov's films," Dr. Robert Colson said, "we can see that they are not the works of a giant but of a midget. Vlasov stole plots from the classics and glorified in the depiction of death and suffering, particularly of women, whom he was incapable of seeing as other than a destroying force or as powerless victims. The sentimental glorification of Mike Vlasov is an adolescent fixation that film scholarship must outgrow."

The tiny, chilled audience of professors and grad students applauded politely. Colson, a tall man in his mid-thirties whose face had turned red during his presentation, smiled in acknowledgement.

Ordinarily, wild horses could not have dragged me to a session titled "Shadows and Torment: The Legacy of Mike Vlasov." However, my other choices were "Star Trek as American Imperialism" and "Gay and Lesbian Subtexts in Gilligan's Island." Not wanting to go back to my motel room so soon, I opted for Vlasov.

The highlight of the session was not finding out about Mike Vlasov, a horror movie producer of the Forties, but seeing Dr. Susan Anbenkian, a thin woman with a dark complexion whose presentation on Vlasov's unrealized projects could not have been better. Ignoring the midwestern chill in the room, she presented as if she had never left Golson State University in California. Her voice hit the perfect note of irony when discussing the odd decisions of Vlasov's bosses and censors, and I decided she was easily the most interesting woman at Taylorville State University's Pop Culture Conference.

"Well, we're almost officially out of time," the chairman said. "I know many of you need to catch that last shuttle. It's been a very informative and interesting session. Thank you."

The underheated room cleared in moments. The chairman and the first presenter, a stout grad student who had stammered through his entire talk, hurried away. Colson's grad students rushed to worship at his feet. I approached Susan Anbenkian.

"Ed Hays, Spartanville State," I said. "Horror movies aren't really my field, but your talk made me realize that I've seen The Black Museum several times. I'm sure your paper took a lot of research."

"Thank you." A smile lit up her face, and my heart beat faster.

"How did you get interested in Vlasov? He sounds like an interesting guy."

She laughed. "I saw The Werdegast Inheritance the summer my aunt got a black-and-white TV with UHF. I thought the idea of a lady werewolf was cool."

"That is an idea that's pretty rare."

She smiled. "Of course, I didn't fully appreciate that movie until I was in my teens. After I discovered boys, that movie really made sense."

I chuckled knowingly. Colson's presentation had beaten the linkage between female sexual desire and lycanthropy in The Werdegast Inheritance into the ground.

"I'd love to hear more about your work," I said. "Were you going to have dinner with anyone tonight?"

She opened her mouth to reply when Colson, his acolytes freshly dismissed, turned to us.

"An interesting paper, Dr. Anbenkian. I didn't know much about Vlasov's unrealized projects, although the material you presented still supports my thesis. I would be delighted to continue our duel at dinner tonight."

"I'm afraid I've already committed to Dr. Hays," she said.

"Hays?" Colson blinked.

"Ed Hays, Spartanville State," I said.

"From Harriet to Edith: Sitcom Wives of the Postwar Era? That Hays?" His eyes narrowed. "Isn't Vlasov a little out of your area?"

"I'm thinking of working on horror in early television," I said, spinning a lie. "Vlasov was a major influence on The Twilight Zone."

Colson seemed flustered for a moment.

"Well, then you can add to our discussion. I know I should know more about television than I do."

I hated to admit it, but Robert Colson looked vulnerable for a moment. If we said no to him, he would be alone with no audience to dazzle, no grad students to humble, no listeners of any kind. He would be simply alone.

I would have left him there, but Susan spoke first.

"Just as long as we pick a nice restaurant for our Vlasov seminar, I'll be happy."

Colson beamed. "Splendid."

We gathered our briefcases and stepped out of the darkening classroom. As we did, a man immediately rushed into the Men's Room beyond the stairs. I couldn't see his face, but I got an impression of a tall man wearing the most hideous paisley tie I had ever seen. Pink and dark blue were locked in mortal combat on his chest, and when I closed my eyes, I could still see the dreadful thing.

"Good Lord, that man must have let his mother dress him," Colson said as we walked down the stairs.

"What man?" Susan asked.

"The one who went into the Men's Room. Wore a horrible paisley tie."

"He wasn't at the session, was he?" I asked.

"I should say not." Colson shuddered. "I couldn't have presented if I had had to look at such a ghastly thing."

"It can't be worse than lecturing to students who wear 'Big Johnson' T-shirts," I said.

"I can't get the damn thing out of my mind." Colson shook his head as if he could dislodge the memory that way.

"I don't remember him at the session," Susan said, "but he should have been there."

I looked puzzled.

"That was one of Vlasov's tricks." She laughed. "He had a collection of bad ties, and he would wear them to meetings with studio executives he especially despised."

"Repressed hostility." Colson made a tsk-tsk sound. "And utterly meaningless as a revolt. Why do you like the man?"

We reached the ground floor and walked out of the Ackley Building into the pale twilight and cruel wind of an early January night. Scattered snowflakes fell, while cars raced along the slick streets, their drivers hoping to get home before the freeze. TSU itself was on break, the conference being shoehorned in at this time, so the campus itself was quite empty.

"Anybody know a good place to eat?" I asked, shuddering at the wind that came in off the Lake. "This is my first time in Taylorville."

"I was walking around last night and found a nice, quiet place," Colson said.

"Quiet is good," Susan said, as she pulled her coat tighter around her Californian body. "Warm would be better."

"It's called the Golden Fountain, and I think it is warm."

He led us up Broad Street's slushy sidewalk for two blocks, then signaled that we were to cross and go up a side street.

"There's no crosswalk here." Susan looked at the road. "Or even a traffic light."

"The nearest one is two blocks farther up." Colson pointed to a red light bobbing on its wires in the distance. "Look, the traffic isn't so bad now. We can just brazen it across."

I looked at the cars driving past on the slick black pavement and disliked the idea of crossing. Still, walking up two more blocks and then back on the other side in this wind held absolutely no appeal. I hadn't needed gloves this morning when I left my motel, but now my fingers were quite cold.

I looked at Colson. He might sound like a jerk, I thought, but he seemed like a guy who could pick a good restaurant.

"Let's risk it," I said.

Susan sighed as if she couldn't believe what we were going to do, but she stayed with us.

We watched the traffic, waiting for our chance. Each time I looked to my left, the glow of the street lamp made me blink, and I could see that hideous paisley.

"Now," Colson ordered, and we hurried into the street. We crossed the first two lanes without problem, paused on the double yellow line, then rushed ahead. Suddenly, a rusty orange Chevy Cavalier barreled through the red light at us.

"Run!"

The Chevy blew its horn as I shouted and pulled Susan forward. I shut my eyes as I ran, for the world turned to paisley. My knee popped, and I screamed. Gasping cold air into my lungs, I opened my eyes and found myself on the sidewalk, as the Chevy driver squealed away.

Susan stood next to me, looking as rattled as I felt. I gave her a smile.

"We won't try that again," I promised.

"It's this way, down here," Colson said, pointing down a side street filled with video stores and laundromats.

Susan and I sighed and followed him past these signs of college life until we came to an old brownstone building that bore the sign "The Golden Fountain."

As soon as I saw it, I relaxed. Indeed, I only now realized how tense I had been since the session had ended, and how I'd been clenching myself like a fist against the cold wind. My tension just drained away, and I hurried over to open the door for Colson and Susan.

Susan's eyes widened as she stepped inside.

"I think I like this place," she said.

A wave of warmth flowed over us as soon as the door closed behind us. The restaurant's namesake splashed noisily in the lobby. A transparent ball with a small human figure inside it bobbed up and down on the plume that leaped from the fountain.

"How many?" a tall woman asked as she stepped out the darkness.

I stared at her and couldn't speak because I thought she was Susan's twin. However, the more I looked at her, the more I marveled that I had ever thought anything so foolish. The hostess was older, wore too much makeup, and seemed vaguely Asian.

"Three," Colson said.

"Follow me."

We followed her to a dark booth lit by three candles on the table. The wallpaper was covered with interlocking arrow crosses, and a black-and-white photo of a man with old-fashioned glasses and thinning hair hung on the wall overlooking us.

"It's what's his name." Colson snapped his fingers and tried to think. "I've seen him in a million movies."

I found myself nodding agreement.

"That's who it is," I said. "Never a star but always in everything."

"That is no actor," the hostess said. Her voice was low and smokey. "That was Mr. Montgomery. A very good friend of Mr. Custic, the founder of the Golden Fountain. A poet, Mr. Montgomery would sit at this table every night and write poetry." She lowered her gaze. "Of course, he is now dead."

We sat down and quickly ordered drinks.

"I don't care what she said, that is an actor." Colson pointed at the photo once the hostess left. "Why can't I remember his name?"

"Dan Duryea," I said.

Susan shook her head in alarm. "That's not Dan Duryea."

"Ed, that most definitely is not Dan Duryea," Colson said. "This guy looks too kind. Duryea's face was always threatening to slip into a sneer."

"It was a good guess." Susan patted my hand. "The photo does have that *film noir* look I associate with Duryea."

A middle-aged waitress arrived with our drinks and took our order. For a place so close to the university, it surprised me that the Golden Fountain seemed to operate entirely without college student labor.

Susan took a sip of wine and laughed.

"It all fits together." She took a second sip as Colson and I stared at her. "The Vlasov session, the man with the tie, and Dan Duryea."

I blinked.

"Duryea played the killer in <u>The Stranger Behind You</u>," she said. "The man who never talks. We see him at his job, with his mother, on the street. He never gets a word in. He only puts this ugly tie on and goes out and strangles people."

"But it was a striped tie," Colson said.

"Probably because a paisley tie wouldn't work well in black-and-white." Susan closed her eyes and shivered. "The only time he talks is right before he dies. 'It can't be helped,' he says and falls out the window."

"Falls out my foot." Colson sneered. "He jumps. They only have the policeman say he fell so they could get the scene past the censor. If you pay attention to the action, you see he jumps on purpose." He looked at me and wagged a finger. "Suicide as a plot solution was a big no-no in those days, Ed."

He turned back to Susan.

"So you're saying that Vlasov modeled the strangler after himself?" He laughed. "That would give me the winning weapon in our argument."

Susan didn't seem at all distressed.

"I think it was meant as a joke. He made <u>The Stranger Behind You</u> only when 'Die Gently, Stranger' fell apart. Thematically, <u>Stranger</u> is the simplest of his late films. He had to make a film quickly to get out of that contract with Universal, and he threw in what he could to make it interesting. Probably having an ugly tie in that movie was his way of thumbing his nose at Universal's bosses for ruining the project he wanted to make."

The waitress brought our meals.

"He could always have quit," Colson said, as he cut into his steak. "Gone back to writing."

"He had a family."

"In southern California at that time, I'm sure he could have found something else to support them. Get in on the ground floor of television."

Time to intervene before blood is shed, I thought.

"I guess you guys have seen all of Vlasov's films."

Both fell silent.

"Not all," Susan said, breaking the silence first. "There is The Ghost Walks."

"Why haven't you watched it?" I asked. "No time? Is it sitting there neglected among your videotapes?"

"It's not on videotape," she said. "The Ghost Walks is a real Hollywood horror story. A new management had come in at Universal, and Vlasov hoped they would let him get away from the horror genre. Instead, they told him his next film would be called The Ghost Walks. In revenge, he made it a romantic fantasy about a poet who falls in love with a ghost."

"It didn't do well at the box office," Colson said, taking over the discussion, "because the title and the subject matter clashed. The studio pulled it from release and then suppressed it when Selznik made Portrait of Jenny. By the time Vlasov had become a cult figure decades later and there was money in his old films…"

"The negative had deteriorated," Susan said. "It's Vlasov's lost film. A shame because it sounds like his most personal project, and all we have are the reviews."

"You've read them, I assume," Colson asked her. "Typical Vlasovian morbidity. The hero is a poet who spends his time mooning about in a restaurant. He never gets the girl, since she's a ghost, and his book of new poems flops."

"If he had gotten the girl, or if his book had sold a million copies, you'd accuse Vlasov of pandering the dream machine's fantasies." Susan smiled, showing her teeth.

"Good shot," I said.

"I wish I could remember that fellow's name," Colson said, looking at the photo again. "I'm sure he's an actor."

He signaled the waitress and asked for the check. I watched Susan finish her wine and imagined her naked and smoking a cigarette after lovemaking. If only I could get rid of Colson.

"The poet is a typical Vlasov character," Colson said as he waited. "The Impotent Observer. They might have charm. They might be intelligent. But they are utterly incapable of taking action. They find themselves immobilized in bad situations. Imprisoned by fate."

The waitress returned.

"Let me take care of this." Colson took out his billfold with a grand lord-of-the-manor air. "Let Vanstartt College take care of this."

A nice way to remind us who taught at the best school, I thought as I let Colson pay up.

The waitress walked away, and I glimpsed a man in the lobby, watching the ball dancing in the golden fountain. Tall and middle-aged, his black hair was tinged with gray and he wore surprisingly thick-lensed glasses of a kind I hadn't seen in real life in years. His shoulders were slightly stooped, and there was an atmosphere of being crushed by life that seemed to cling to him as he studied the movement of that ball dancing in the water.

He turned a bit, and his paisley tie, his hideous paisley tie, snapped into focus.

"It's him," I said, putting my hand on Colson's wrist and interrupting another of his monologues. "The man with the tie."

"Well, I'll be damned." Colson stared at the man. "Look at those glasses. They must have gone out of style when Eisenhower was President."

The man, his face unreadable, now looked directly at us. I thought I saw anger there but some pity as well. Anger, however, seemed to win out.

"Who does he think he is, looking at us like that?" Colson glanced at me for approval and then looked back at the man. "I'm going to give him a piece of my mind."

"Skip it," Susan said. "Let him stare."

"I think you should confront him," I said. If Colson got tangled up with this guy, I could finally get Susan Anbenkian to myself.

Colson squared his shoulders, got up and strode over to the lobby. I turned to Susan.

"Alone at last. Would you like to share a cab back to the motel?"

"Only if the fare is split three ways."

"In that case, why not let Vanstartt College take care of the taxi? They have more money than Spartanville and Golson State put together."

A little pity, enough to hurt, seeped into her expression.

"Is life really that bad? You get paid for studying television, you know."

Just then, Colson ran over to us.

"I've just seen the strangest thing," he said. "You've got to come out here and tell me if you remember this from when we came in."

Frowning, I threw my napkin on the table and followed him.

"Did you talk to Mr. Tie?" I asked.

"He ran away before I could speak to him. But after he left, I saw this."

Colson pointed to a poster advertising "The Black Museum – See It If You Dare."

I didn't remember the poster from when we entered the Golden Fountain, but I had the uncomfortable feeling I had seen it before somewhere. I turned to Susan, who looked as if she had seen Banquo's ghost.

And then I knew where I had seen it before.

"It's the same," she said. She ran her finger over it. "Is it a poster for the movie?"

Colson stepped over for a closer look.

"No. There's no credits like there would be on a movie poster." He pointed at the bottom. "And here's an address and map." He studied it for a moment. "If it is a real place, it shouldn't be far from here."

Susan's raised her eyebrows.

"It's less than a block," the hostess said. "You should see it. It's fascinating."

Colson pointed at the poster. "Did they make this after the movie came out?"

"Movie?" The hostess was puzzled. "I don't go to the cinema much." She stepped to the door and pointed. "You can find the museum easily. Just walk out to the right, cut through the alley to Keith Street, and there it is."

Susan looked at her watch.

"It has to be closed, though. It's after seven."

"Oh, no. On Friday nights he keeps it open late."

"Who does?" Susan asked.

"Mr. Helpmann. He eats here a lot."

Mr. Helpmann? That was the proprietor's name in the movie. His name conjured up a thin little man who looked like Heinrich Himmler. He viewed the world with disdain through his round-lensed glasses and finally killed his wife and ended up as an exhibit in his own museum.

The first time I saw The Black Museum, Helpmann really got under my skin. For nights after that, I dreamed about him watching me with those protected eyes, weighing and dissecting my faults.

The name affected Susan and Colson as well. Susan looked amazed, as if she had just learned that Shangri-La could be found behind the McDonald's on the corner. Colson, on the other hand, puckered his lips and seemed ready to explode.

"We have to go," I said. "This is all too good to pass up. A Black Museum run by a Mr. Helpmann? The guy behind it has to be a lunatic Vlasov fan. Can you imagine it? Going there would be the perfect end to our Vlasov evening."

Colson sighed. "It's obviously just a tourist trap." He shook his head. "Ed, if you want to go, you can go, but I think Susan and I will go back to the motel like sensible people."

"Well, I think I want to go to the Black Museum," Susan said. "This 'Helpmann' has to be the biggest Vlasov fan of all time."

"If you put it like that, I suppose it might be fun to see how far Vlasovmania can drive some people," Colson said. "Although I think the guy must be on the verge of losing his shirt."

The hostess stared daggers at us.

"How do we get there?" I asked her.

"Out onto the sidewalk and turn right. Take the alley over to Keith Street. You can't miss the Black Museum then."

I pushed the door open and waited for Susan and Colson. Before I let the door swing shut, I noticed the human figure in the ball splashing at the top of the fountain. He looked happy, but he was at the mercy of forces he couldn't control or understand.

"Do you really want to see this silliness?" Colson asked Susan as he pulled at his collar and shivered in the night wind.

"That's what she said," I said and stepped in front of them. "On to the Black Museum."

A glance over my shoulder showed me they were both following me. That was good because I instantly regretted my boldness. I couldn't believe the hostess had told us to go through an alley. Taylorville wasn't East Keokuk, after all. I had no desire to get killed walking to some trashy museum.

The night didn't ease my fears either. Taylorville seemed to have streetlights that only cast a sickly orange light into the winter blackness. My stomach tightened, and I wanted to turn back, but I knew Susan would write me off completely if I did.

I kept walking. The alley loomed to the right. A large man stood at its mouth, watching us approach. He suddenly turned, letting the light strike his ugly paisley tie. After smiling, he walked into the alley's shadows.

"Guys," I said, my voice a bare whisper.

"Susan, what's your favorite part of The Black Museum?" Colson asked.

"The scene in which Helpmann walks through the museum for the last time, turning the lights off over each exhibit. You just know he's going to kill his wife." She chuckled. "We *know* something awful is going to happen, and it can't be stopped."

"And you think that makes Vlasov an artist?" Colson asked. He laughed. "I admit a guilty pleasure of mine is the murder scene itself. Darkness cut by the flashing neon light outside the window. A perfectly pretentious effort to dress garbage up as art."

"Let's talk about something else," I said as we entered the alley.

"What's your favorite part, Ed?" Colson asked.

A bus's airbrakes hissed behind us out on the street. I jumped and turned to look, and Susan grinned at my distress.

It took me a while to get my breath back.

"I guess I like the first story, about Peter the Great's torturer."

I turned around and resumed walking forward. A light shut off in the building to the left, and I could hear the scrape of someone opening a window. I looked up to see who was watching us, but all I could make out was a tall, mannish shape.

Did it have a paisley tie, or was that my imagination?

A cat wailed from over to my right. I walked faster, hoping it wasn't black and that it wouldn't run in front of me.

"The violence in that murder scene is incredible for its time," Colson said. "The hatred that Helpmann must feel toward his wife…"

A light turned on over a doorway to my right. The man with the tie stepped beneath the light and looked at me. I couldn't mistake his expression now. It was one of hatred. His cheeks were sucked in, his lips pouted slightly, and his eyes just burned with anger.

I ran ahead into the darkness, and more lights snapped on. I turned to my left and saw my shadow. It reminded me of a movie image. Who was behind the light watching me?

A movie image couple walked onto this "screen," holding hands.

"Helpmann is the character who is Vlasov," Colson said. "He's eaten up with self-loathing. Vlasov isn't the impotent observer, like the ticket seller in The Black Museum or the poet in The Ghost Walks." He waved his hand. "His apologists would like us to think so, and Vlasov fed them plenty of lines during his life, but the more you know about him, you know Vlasov is always the menace. Always the killer."

It was the passion that made them a couple, I thought as I saw them together. They shared a passion for these old black-and-white films from before they were born that fewer and fewer people felt. They didn't agree on how to read these films, but something in those images ignited a passion in them.

I couldn't feel that passion.

I realized that I was walking down the alley, terrified of who knew what behind those lights, and it was all for nothing. I would never have Susan. She had more in common with Colson than with me.

The man with the tie now stepped into the light, walking toward us with a deliberate pace that would not be stopped. I ran out onto Keith Street and looked up and down for a cab.

And then I saw it, the Black Museum.

It was just a typical, box-like brick structure. Three stories tall, it had a red neon sign running down its front – THE BLACK MUSEUM   S E IT IF YOU DARE – that flashed on and off, casting its light into the proprietor's bedroom just like in the movie. As I stared at it, I could imagine the color draining out of the scene. It could only exist as a film noir.

"It is the same sign. Even the E in see is burned out." Susan chuckled. "This guy must really be living some Mike Vlasov fantasy."

Colson just stared in amazement. He opened his mouth to make some witty comment, no doubt, but words, for once, failed him. He just stood there on the sidewalk as the man with the hideous tie stepped closer.

"This place has to be unbelievable," he said at last. "Let's go in."

We hurried across Keith Street, not even having to dodge traffic. We climbed five steps to the door and entered to the lobby. The ticket booth was empty. I stepped away from Susan and Colson to examine a postcard stand. I gave it a twirl, and it squeaked loudly. The cards showed cheesy dummies performing ghastly deeds of mayhem. I recognized the stories from the movie: Peter the Great, the Demon-Barber, Bluebeard. Still, I kept thinking of the man with the tie outside.

"My clerk is nowhere to be found."

I nearly jumped at the strange voice behind me.

"How many please?"

I turned and thought I was looking at Heinrich Himmler. A man with slumped shoulders, round-lensed glasses and a thin, worm-like moustache stood in the middle of the lobby and regarded me with contempt.

"Mr. Helpmann?" Susan could barely whisper.

He turned to her, and his face became even more unpleasant.

"Have we met?" he asked.

I pulled out my wallet. "Three tickets please."

He took my money with bad grace, let himself into the ticket booth, and tore three tickets.

"There you are." He handed me the stubs. "Enter through that door. Smoking is not allowed."

"Of course," I said, thinking it was odd he should have to say something so obvious, before I noticed the large ashtrays on either side of the door.

Did people still expect to smoke in public places, I wondered.

"Come on, you two," Colson said. He laughed, a bit too loudly. "Let's go get the fright of our lives."

Susan followed, but I felt rooted to the floor. Colson pulled my arm, while Helpmann watched us, piggish contempt on his face.

"Come on, Ed," Colson said, pulling me into the darkness beyond the door. "Helpmann's just some nut."

I didn't want to go into the dark, but I didn't want to look foolish in front of Susan either. I took a deep breath and walked forward, but not fast enough for Colson, who said, in his best Hitchcock voice:

"It's only a movie."

I froze again.

"What's wrong now?" Anger simmered in Colson's voice.

"What you said. It's only a movie. It's a movie."

Colson sighed. "Surely you've heard that before."

"You don't understand. It is a movie. We're in The Black Museum."

"Of course we are." Colson shook his head. "Yes, Ed, you paid for the tickets, and now we can go through the museum."

"Not the place," I said. "The movie. We're in the movie The Black Museum itself. This place will be set up exactly like it was in the movie. Peter the Great first, then a Newgate hanging, then Sweeney Todd."

"How the hell can we be in a movie?" Colson asked.

"We are. The first exhibit will be Peter the Great."

We turned the corner and found ourselves in a torture chamber dominated by an enraged giant of a man with shoulder-length black hair and a dashing moustache. He glared at two cringing torturers, one of whom looked aghast at a blonde female head on the floor.

The sign on the railing meant to prevent us from getting too close read PETER THE GREAT. Something shapeless hung next to the sign.

Susan stepped up to the railing.

"It is just like the movie," she said. Then she looked down and unwrapped the thing next to the sign. She gasped and held it out to us in the pale light.

A paisley tie.

Colson began to laugh. A nervous laugh that didn't stop and climbed higher and higher as it became breathless.

And then he turned and ran.

Susan and I rushed after him. Mr. Helpmann stood at the ticket window, a grimly disapproving look on his face as we burst from darkness into light. I glanced at him and saw that he was polishing a butcher knife.

I rushed outside, Susan behind me, and we ran down the steps to Keith Street as Colson entered the alley.

"Damn it!"

I turned around and saw that Susan's shoe had lost a heel.

"I'll get him," I said, and I ran across the street into the alley.

Colson had stopped running beneath a harsh white light a few yards ahead of me. The man with the tie loomed over him, only now the tie was around Colson's neck, being pulled as tightly as the other man could yank it.

"It can't be helped," the man with the tie said.

Colson writhed, and I could see his tongue, his brilliant, sarcastic tongue, trapped between his teeth. The tongue that had, ever so cleverly, speared and condemned the career of Mike Vlasov, was now half bitten-through, bloody and dead.

As Mike Vlasov let Colson's body hit the pavement, I realized it was the second time I had seen Colson die this evening. The first time had been when that rusty Chevy Cavalier plowed into us as he tried to cross Broad Street.

I turned back to Susan, remembering her scream as the Chevy's bumper slammed into her hips. Now she stood on Keith Street, embraced by a sudden fog. I could barely make her out as a dark shape in the midst of the white, when I heard the clip-clop of horses' hooves approach.

She raised her hands to her head and tried to scream, and I wanted to run to her and hold her, but I had the feeling she was in another movie.

Pulled by two black horses, a coach moved between Susan and me. A footman, in Eighteenth Century livery, dismounted and opened the door for her. The fog parted enough for me to make out the Werdegast coat-of-arms on the door of the coach. Susan entered and waved to me before the whiteness rolled over everything, and the clip-clop sound resumed.

A firm hand clutched my shoulder. I turned and looked up. Mike Vlasov, tieless, regarded me with tired eyes.

I wanted to run, and I realized I didn't know where to run. Into the Gothic past? Into the *noir* present? Into the real world where I lay dead on a slick Taylorville street?

Vlasov studied my face carefully, always squeezing my shoulder tighter.

"It can't be helped," I said.

The ghost of a smile crossed his face, and he pushed me forward, across a now fogless Keith Street, to return me to the Black Museum.

I understood. He didn't really hate me, not the way he hated Colson. I had just gotten caught up in things I didn't understand. I was like that guy in the ball in the fountain, bounced around by forces I knew nothing about.

As he opened the door to the Black Museum for me, I realized it could be worse. Granted, I would not live in aristocratic comfort like Susan, but I wouldn't turn into a werewolf either. Unlike Colson, I wouldn't be a victim, dying over and over again whenever anyone watched the movie.

No, I would be what Colson had called an impotent observer. I wouldn't be killed, but I wouldn't kill either. I would simply watch, unable to do anything, while those around me acted out their dark dramas.

Vlasov released me, and I walked over to the ticket booth. Mr. Helpmann sneered as I approached him.

"Late again, Mr. Hays. I've had to take care of the customers tonight. That's not what I pay you for."

"No, Mr. Helpmann," I said, and I silently took my place behind the ticket counter. Helpmann pressed his finger into my chest.

"Always remember who's in charge of this museum," he said.

The door opened, and customers filed into the lobby, eager to see the latest exhibit of man's inhumanity to man, a death mask of the tie murderer's latest victim. Next to the postcard stand, ignored by everyone, Mike Vlasov adjusted his paisley tie and looked at me.

"I will remember, Mr. Helpmann," I said. "I will remember who's in charge of this museum."

Mike Vlasov nodded at my words, sighed, then turned and walked outside into the shadows and torment.

The Man Who Knew Karloff

As Cindy stepped into the room, Mr. Morozov sat by the window, soaking up the precious January sunlight. He looked at his scrapbook and did not raise his bald head. Cindy wondered if he had heard her enter.

She walked between the two beds, rolled up Mr. Walker's sleeve and put on the cuff to take his blood pressure. Mr. Walker continued to lie in bed and watch something a mile beyond the ceiling.

Cindy sighed as she inflated the cuff. Working on 4-B was different from 2-C. There, most of the people had been healthy and happy. Here, everyone was either at death's door or had been moved from other floors because of problems.

She heard Mr. Morozov turn a page and say "Ah!" It was the first happy sound she had heard on 4-B in a week. She looked at the smiling bald man. All the other nurses insisted that Morozov was crazy. She hadn't seen any proof of that so far.

After taking note of Mr. Walker's blood pressure, she undid the cuff. The Velcro's ripping sound made Mr. Morozov look at her.

"Dobri den," he said and rolled up his sleeve.

"You know I don't understand that." She laughed and put the cuff on him.

"Good day is what it means. That's all. You will now tell the other nurses that I am a crazy old man?" He regarded her with piercing blue eyes until she blushed. He smiled and nodded to himself.

Eager to escape his gaze, Cindy looked down at his notebook. A familiar face, upside down, smiled at her. She blinked twice and then remembered the name.

"Boris Karloff."

"Ah." Mr. Morozov lifted a finger and shook it at her. "You're not as young as you pretend. Tomorrow, perhaps, they will lock you in here too."

XXX

"I met a real interesting patient today," Cindy said as she took the lasagna out of the oven and set it on top of the stove.

Her brother Dick grunted from the kitchen table and looked out the window at the Toyota in the Wallicki's driveway.

"That's why the country is going to hell. Everybody's buying Japanese cars. In ten years, the Japs'll be running this country. See if I'm not right."

Cindy sighed. That was Dick's idea of talk, mimicking what Dad used to say. She tried to start the conversation again.

"He knew Boris Karloff." Cindy put the lasagna down on the cork pad in the center of the kitchen table. Dick turned to look at her.

"No shit? Somebody at Bright Acres knew a movie star?"

Cindy smiled and started cutting. "He said Karloff was very nice." She met Dick's eyes. "A real gentleman."

"What, did he work with him on Frankenstein?"

"No. Mr. Morozov worked with him on Dark Reflection. He was the nephew of the producer, Mike Vlasov."

Dick made a raspberry and turned back to the window. "Everybody talks about how great Vlasov's movies are, but they're a lot of nothing. I saw a couple at TSU last year, and they bored me shitless."

Cindy put her knife down and kneaded her right hand with her left. "I've invited him over for Friday night dinner. I know how much you like horror movies."

"Yeah, *horror* movies. Movies where stuff actually happens, like <u>Halloween</u>, not where they sit around for 90 minutes talking if somebody really turns into a wolf or only thinks that she turns into a wolf and then when the lights come up you sit there and think 'what the fuck was that all about?'"

Cindy had picked up the spatula and aimed it at the incision in the lasagna. Then she closed her eyes, snorted out her breath, and slammed the spatula down on the table.

"Dammit, I think Mr. Morozov is interesting. I thought it would be good to have him over on Friday. I thought you would like it. And since I'm the one who brings money into this house, guess what? He's going to come over on Friday night."

Dick looked at her and bit his lip. After he counted to ten, he pouted. "When I graduate from TSU, I'll be making the money. Big bucks. Bring your old fart over on Friday night. Just don't expect me to be impressed."

Cindy stuck the spatula into the lasagna, which gave a wet wheeze as she worked a section loose. When she slapped it on Dick's plate, a drop of tomato sauce his white Taylorville State University sweatshirt.

XXX

"It's good to see the night," Mr. Morozov said, staring up at the stars in the chill twilight. He watched his steamy breath rise like smoke from an offering fire. "It has been so long."

"Get inside before you get cold." Cindy shut the car door and put an arm around him to propel him to the house. "I have to take care of you tonight."

They walked up the porch of the duplex and could hear muffled TV noises. When Cindy opened the door, the sounds of "Newscenter Seven" became clear. She sighed and hoped that Dick wouldn't go on about that black anchorwoman's bosom in front of Mr. Morozov.

She motioned down the hall, to the source of the volume. "That's my brother Dick in there. Go in and say 'hi'."

Removing his fur hat and gloves, Mr. Morozov walked to the living room. Cindy stepped into the dark kitchen. She snapped the light on and looked at the oven, hoping that Dick had remembered to put the casserole in as she had asked, but she feared that he had forgotten.

The oven sat cold and empty.

She cursed under the sound of the traffic report and turned the oven on, and then pulled the casserole from the fridge. She prayed that the evening would improve.

"So you're the guy who knew Karloff?" she could hear Dick ask.

"Yes. I am Andrew Morozov."

No one said anything as Cindy ran to the living room. Once there, she grabbed the knob and cut down the TV's volume by half.

"I was very thrilled to work with Karloff," Mr. Morozov said. "He was famous, and I was so young. I thought – here he is, a Russian who has made a success in Hollywood." He chuckled. "Of course, he wasn't a Russian at all but an Englishman."

"Yeah, I know," Dick said, shifting on the sofa to see the TV screen better. "I've read Famous Monsters of Filmland."

"Is that why you forgot to put the casserole in the oven?" Cindy asked. "You were reading Famous Monsters of Filmland?"

"I forgot, okay. People forget things every day. I had a big test in Poli Sci this morning that I bombed, and I forgot about the stupid casserole."

Mr. Morozov coughed. "Something to drink, please, if it isn't any trouble."

Thankful for the distraction, Cindy led the old man out to the kitchen and poured him some wine.

"If you were in Hollywood, why did you ever come to Taylorville?" she asked. "I wouldn't mind if I never saw another winter."

He guest smiled. "A Morozov needs the winter, you know." He watched her blank expression, then shrugged at his failed joke and regarded the dull red liquid in his glass. He raised it to let the light from the ceiling lamp shine through it.

"And there were other things. Hollywood is not so pleasant a place. It killed my Uncle Misha after all."

"I always thought making movies would be fun."

"I could be fun," he said and put the glass down on the table. He smiled at her. "There was the time I saved <u>Dark Reflection</u>."

"That one had Karloff."

He pointed at her. "That movie wouldn't exist without me. It began as 'The Last Manderville,' with Karloff as a deranged aristocrat. The director had never directed a movie before. He was a writer, a talented writer Uncle Mischa had promoted to the chair, but he fell hopelessly behind schedule. Then, to make things worse, Karloff hurt his back while filming his death scene."

"But that must have been at the end of the movie anyway."

Mr. Morozov shook his head. "It wasn't, and a pirate movie needed the Eighteenth Century costumes and sets at once. There was no chance to wait around for Karloff to recover. We had no star and half of the picture left to shoot. What could Uncle Misha do? He only had half a film."

Mr. Morozov stood up in the center of the kitchen and made a gathering gesture around him. "He called his team together and said 'Kids, we're in a jam. A thousand dollars for the best way out of it.'" Mr. Morozov began to pace. "All that night, I asked myself, what is to be done to save this picture?"

He turned to Cindy and snapped his fingers. It sounded like a gunshot.

"I had it! Karloff's Squire Manderville was quite vain, always near a mirror, always regarding himself. He had even contrived to die hear a mirror. What if one of those mirrors, I asked himself, turned up in the present, with his spirit trapped inside?

"Well, Uncle Misha kissed me and gave me the thousand dollars. He came up with a contemporary story, we needed no expensive sets, Karloff did some narration from his hospital bed to tie things together, and we had a movie."

"A pretty boring one," Dick said from the doorway. "I mean Karloff's death was okay, and the way the couple in New York died was okay, but you had to wait until nearly the whole movie was over before something happened. I almost walked out when I saw Dark Reflection at TSU last year."

Mr. Morozov faced Dick, smiled and bowed his head. "I am sorry if my efforts failed to entertain you. What movies do you prefer?"

"Halloween. Dawn of the Dead." Dick looked at Cindy's frown and raised his hands. He turned back to Morozov. "Hey, I mean it wasn't your fault that you guys weren't working in color back then, but you could have showed more."

"No doubt we should have, but we had to deal with a censor. Still, it is probably fortunate that my uncle died when he did, rather than live and be dismissed as a dinosaur."

"Well, at least he set some of his movies in America and not in some bullshit Transylvania." Dick walked over to the refrigerator and took out a can of Mountain Dew. "When's supper going to be ready?"

"About an hour," Cindy said after a pause.

"Cool." Dick walked back to the TV.

Mr. Morozov sat down and drank his wine. Cindy turned to the silverware drawer and gathered the flatware. The metal clattered as she spoke.

"They have a good film society at TSU. Would you have liked to have seen your uncle's movies when they showed them last year?"

Mr. Morozov opened his mouth, then closed it. His brow furrowed, and he rocked in the chair. "I'm not sure," he finally said.

"Why?"

Again, the old man furrowed his brow. Finally he held out his hands to her.

"For you to watch my uncle's movies, it is different. You would only see stories and characters." He put his hands over his heart. "I, however, would see and remember friends. Karloff, Dan Duryea, and others. I would remember those off camera as well, my uncle, the cameraman, the script girls. All dead now. I would remember them all and think 'How much longer until I join them?'"

"I never thought of it like that."

"It is a question that is always before me." Mr. Morozov shrugged. "Yet I remember the power of those films. Seeing an audience jump as one person or fall silent because of what my uncle did. To watch hundreds of people sitting still, forgetting even to chew popcorn, thinking the same thought because of what he did." He laughed. "The power is immense. Godlike."

He stood up and clapped his hands.

"To feel that power once more would be magnificent."

XXX

"So, something happen at work today?" Dick asked before he put a forkful of spaghetti in his mouth.

"One of the patients died." Cindy looked out the window.

Dick snorted.

"Well, I figured it had to be something like that, you being so talkative tonight and everything." Dick shook more cheese on his spaghetti. "Which geezer was it? One of the ones you liked?"

"Mr. Morozov." Cindy looked at Dick for a response. "We had him over that one time, remember?"

Dick had no response. Cindy sighed.

"He had a heart attack during the night and died."

"Well, he had to be pretty old, if he knew Karloff, I mean."

Cindy licked her lips and then grabbed her brother's arm.

"I took his scrapbook. I've never taken anything from a patient before, but when I came on shift, they told me that he had died. I remembered that scrapbook that made him so happy, and I rushed down to the room to see. They had taken his body away, but his stuff was still there. I saw the scrapbook, and I just grabbed it."

She pressed the back of her hand against her mouth.

"He didn't have any relatives left. It would just have been thrown away. That would have been a shame, I thought. I mean, I think there were letters in there from Karloff and his uncle, Mike Vlasov." She sighed. "It's all about his movie days. Do you think there's any value in it?"

Dick closed his mouth and looked at his sister as if seeing her for the first time.

"Sure that thing's worth money." He began rapping his thumb on the table, a fast rock beat. "That Hollywood nostalgia shit's worth a lot. Plenty of people, especially those that eat from the left side of the plate, will pay big money for something like that. Taking that scrapbook was the best idea you've had in a long time.

"The idiots," Sheldon Witz said, as he looked at the mounted posters he had just unpacked. "I'm dealing with idiots."

He had ordered some old RKO posters, mostly Fred & Ginger stuff. The idiots had sent him RKO posters, only for Mike Vlasov horror movies.

The bell rang as the shop door opened. An overweight college kid in a TSU vinyl jacket paused in the doorway, letting in the winter breeze.

Sheldon sighed. "Can I help you before you let all the heat out?"

"Yeah. You buy movie stuff, right?"

Sheldon fought the urge to say 'No, this is a delicatessen.' He nodded instead. "Sometimes."

The college kid stepped inside and finally let the door close.

"Mostly I sell memorabilia," Sheldon said. "It's hard to find good Hollywood memorabilia in Taylorville. I have to order it from Hollywood."

The college kid gestured at the posters up on the walls. "Mostly musicals, I see." He looked at Sheldon. "It figures."

"So what are you going to sell me? One sheets? Standups?"

"A scrapbook." The kid unsnapped his jacket and put the book on the counter.

Sheldon's eyebrows went up.

"A scrapbook?"

"It has stuff about Karloff in it." The kid opened it up and flipped the pages to a photo of Karloff and some men at a table in a restaurant.

Impressed despite himself, Sheldon leaned forward. He read the neatly-printed names underneath every person.

"So that's Mike Vlasov the genius horror producer! Funny thing now…"

"So how much is it worth? A thousand bucks?"

Sheldon stepped back.

"This isn't the kind of thing I usually handle."

"Seven hundred," the kid said.

Sheldon Witz stared at the kid and tried to take everything in. This schmo hadn't shaved in a while, and his eyes were red. Drugs? Sheldon wondered. Still, there was something in this scrapbook, he thought.

"Let me look some more," he asked and flipped over a few more pages.

An inscription from Mike Vlasov caught his eye.

"You related to Mike Vlasov?" Sheldon asked.

"No," the kid said. "Well, yeah, he was my uncle, or my father's uncle, whatever that makes him to me."

Sheldon Witz bit his lip. And I'm Samuel Goldwyn's bastard, he thought.

"Look," he said. "Since you're related to Mike Vlasov, maybe you'd like to buy some posters from his movies. I got them today, special order."

He picked up one of the posters for <u>Dark Reflection</u> that those idiots had sent him. Karloff's face glowered in a mirror above the lettering.

"I suppose you could think of this as a family heirloom, couldn't you?" he asked, as he showed it to the kid.

The college kid's face went white as he stared at the poster. He grabbed the scrapbook and ran to the door, running out into the cold without a word.

"What the hell?"

Sheldon put the poster down and walked over to close the door. "Crazy kid," he said.

Shaking his head, he walked back to the poster and looked down at a smiling Fred Astaire and Ginger Rogers in Top Hat.

No wonder the kid ran out on me, Sheldon thought. He'd have to think I must be crazy if I can't tell Fred Astaire from Boris Karloff.

XXX

"So how'd the night go?" Cindy asked Ann as she sat down at the table.

Ann shrugged.

"Okay. At least nobody died."

Cindy took a sip of coffee. "Were you the one who found Mr. Morozov the other morning?"

Ann made a disgusted face. "That was a real nightmare. Did you know he died watching an old horror movie?"

Cindy frowned.

"Really? I didn't think he liked to watch those."

"It was playing on the TV. Morozov's dead in the bed, it's that time of night right before the sun rises, so everything's dark, and there's Boris Karloff's face big as life on the TV." Ann shuddered. "I couldn't shut the thing off fast enough. I've seen dead ones before, but having that horror stuff running on the TV made it worse."

"I'm sure," Cindy said.

Ann shut her eyes. "That dead guy's in the bed, and Karloff kept saying, 'You'll never be free. You'll never be free.'"

XXX

Dick hated taking the downtown bus, but that had been the only way to get to that dumb movie shop. Now he had to ride it home.

At the stop after he got on, a woman got on with her slack-jawed son. They took the seat behind Dick. The kid, a real moron as far as Dick could tell, could only talk about watching <u>Frankenstein</u> on Channel 42 tonight. His mom said that Boris Karloff had been a good actor.

"Karloff," the moron said. "Karrrlofff. Karloff Frankenstein. Karloff Frankenstein. Karloff Frankenstein."

His voice ran nails down Dick's mental blackboard. After several blocks, a seat opened up next to a black high school kid. Dick rushed over and sat down.

The black kid looked at Dick for a moment, then turned back to the book he'd been reading, a library copy of <u>Classics of the Horror Film</u>.

Dick glanced at it and couldn't look away. The book lay open to a page on <u>Dark Reflection</u>. Karloff, dagger raised, glared from within a mirror.

This can't be happening, Dick told himself.

The black kid chuckled and tapped his finger against Karloff's scowl.

"You ever see this one? Man, he was evil in that. Evil."

Dick forced himself to smile and turn away.

"Those people who got that mirror in that movie," the kid said. "They had a chance. He was evil. Just evil."

Dick grunted something and looked away. Mercifully, the kid's stop was the next one, and he got up and took his library book with him. A woman with a winter jacket over her waitress uniform got on and sat next to Dick. She ignored him and got out her compact.

After inspecting her face, she began to close the compact when the bus hit a pothole, and everything bounced. The compact slipped from her hand and hit the floor next to Dick's foot.

Dick noticed the waitress looking at him like he was supposed to pick it up. He frowned at her and wanted to ask if she hadn't she ever heard of women's lib. But he decided it probably wasn't worth it, so he leaned down to get it.

"Here you go," he said as he handed it to her.

The compact sprang open.

The glass inside had cracked. In the instant before the woman squeezed the compact shut and slipped it back into her handbag, Dick knew that the cracked mirror had not reflected the bus's interior. For when he had looked into that broken glass, he had seen the fragmented reflection of an old Gothic room, where guttering candleflames danced near dark curtains and a crazed dandy with unruly white hair and a disheveled cravat cackled over the body of his faithless wife.

"Karloff Frankenstein, Karloff Frankenstein," the slack-jawed kid chanted as his mother led him past.

A chill made Dick shudder.

XXX

Dick huffed as he walked up the driveway. The damn scrapbook felt like a ton now. Sweat plastered Dick's hair to his forehead, and his underarms felt wet. A shower, he thought, would be the best thing.

He unlocked the door and turned on the hallway light. Nothing happened. He sighed and leaned against the doorjamb. One more thing to do. Change the stupid lightbulb. Cindy never realized all he did for her.

He walked into the house and let the door close behind him. Standing in the late afternoon murk, he listened. Something in the house sounded different. After a moment, he realized the refrigerator wasn't running.

"Shit." He'd have to fool around with the fuse box. The whole evening had gone to hell. No hot water for a shower now either.

Dick clumped into the darkening kitchen and dropped the scrapbook on the table. Cindy always kept two candles on the table, as if she were trying to impress somebody, but Dick couldn't remember where she kept the matches. He began pulling drawers open, only to slam them shut when he found no matches. The fifth drawer proved lucky, and he was able to light the candles.

He carried one with him as he went to the toilet. Passing the living room, he felt a sudden urge to try the TV. He got halfway to the set when he realized the foolishness of what he was trying to do.

"Of all the stupid ideas," he said, but his hand still reached out to flip the off/on button.

A cheery hum filled the room the moment he did so, reminding Dick of the old black-and-white set his parents had had for so long. The screen before him now filled with picture far more slowly than it should have, but Dick found himself eager to see what the image would be as he stood in the gathering darkness.

The Frankenstein Monster tossed the little girl into the lake.

Chilled, Dick stepped back and closed his eyes.

"I hope you're happy, jerk," he said, thinking of the slack-jawed kid. Dick left the set on and went to the bathroom.

As he walked down the hall, he wondered why the TV should work when all the rest of the appliances were out, but the fact that Frankenstein was on just like that gooney kid had said it would be relaxed him. The late afternoon movie would end soon, and then Gilligan's Island would come on like it always did.

The sounds of the mob burning the windmill cheered him, and he walked out of the bathroom whistling, nearly as jolly as the old Baron, who raised a glass to toast his son's upcoming marriage.

The image on the TV went snowy. It cleared to reveal a wigged Karloff standing before a mirror, admiring an extravagant cravat. "A man's mirror," Karloff said to the glass with a leer, "knows everything about him."

Dick ran to the TV and hit the off/on button. It clicked over to "off," but Karloff remained on screen, ogling his newly arrived country cousin. Dick ran his thumb over the button back and forth, but Dark Reflection continued to play.

He grabbed the dial for the volume and turned it all the way down. It made no difference to the sound of the voices.

Dick turned his back on the screen. The room had become dark, except for the glow from his candle. The other candle still glowed in the kitchen, beckoning him. He began to walk toward it.

"And did you think you could cheat me, my good man?" Squire Manderville asked. "I know what is mine, and those who steal from me know that I never let go of what is mine."

Gripping his candle, Dick walked down the hallway. With his free arm, he reached out in front of him. He swung his arm back and forth, in case someone waited for him in the dark.

His right foot thudded into a stair, and he stopped. There were no stairs in this hallway. He knew that. He had lived in this house all his life, and there had never been stairs in the hallway. Yet there was one in front of him now.

He looked up the stairs. An orange glow beckoned above him. Dick looked back at the grey light behind him. Squire Manderville still spoke.

It wasn't Squire Manderville, he told himself. It was only Boris Karloff, a dead actor in an old movie, safely imprisoned behind the glass of a TV screen.

Dick's nostrils twitched. He smelled a fire, and after a moment he could smell the Squire's wet hunting dogs too. A chill ran down his back. Was there a censor now, he wondered, to make sure that things didn't get too gruesome, to hold the dark impulses of this story in check?

He began to climb the stairs.

XXX

It was good to be home, Cindy thought, as she fished around for her house key. Why hadn't Dick left the porch light on for her? What a selfish jerk, she thought.

She opened the door into darkness. After a moment, she noticed a glow in the kitchen. She stepped inside and closed the door behind her. Voices murmured from the living room. The TV, she supposed.

Cindy walked to the kitchen. There sat Dick, staring past the two short candles at God-knew-what. He almost looked like he was ready to be a patient at Bright Acres. With a sigh, Cindy reached to snap on the kitchen light.

"It won't work," Dick said.

Cindy flipped the switch. No light came on.

"I'll call the power company," she said.

"The phone's dead." Dick looked at her as she picked up the receiver. "Dead."

There was no dial tone.

"It's as dead as that old guy, the one who knew Karloff." Dick chuckled. "Maybe it's deader."

"Did you sell the scrapbook?"

"No." Dick blinked and looked at it lying on the table, as if seeing it for the first time.

"I'll burn it," he said.
"What?"

Dick stood up, grabbed the scrapbook and started to walk to the side of the silent refrigerator. "I'll burn it in the fireplace."

"What fireplace?"

Dick pointed at the wall.

"There's nothing there," Cindy said.

"It's his book," Dick said, nearly trembling. "Don't you see? I have to be free of him."

Cindy grabbed the scrapbook away from her brother. "I took this, and you said it was worth money. I don't know what's wrong with you now, but you're acting like you're stoned, and I won't let you burn this book. I can just hear you blaming me once you sober up."

Dick hit her across the face.

Cindy let go of the scrapbook and stumbled back against the sink. Her left arm flew back and knocked down the carving knife rack. Her hand closed around the grip of the thickest blade.

Her brother knelt to pick up the scrapbook. He opened it, and flipped the pages. A single page stood upright.

"Gotta burn this thing."

He got up and turned back to the table, to the candles. Cindy stepped behind him and raised the knife. She wanted to shove the thick blade into his spine, but part of her rebelled at this urge, and she dropped the knife.

Hearing the clatter, Dick turned around, and Cindy grabbed the scrapbook from him.

"No!" Dick grabbed Cindy by her shoulders. "We have to burn his book. We'll never be free of him otherwise, Cindy. Don't you see that?"

His hands closed around her throat. Before she knew it, he was choking her. She kicked at him as her head shook back and forth. He kept squeezing. Cindy bit her tongue and stared at the cheery fireplace on the wall.

She closed her eyes and went limp. Dickon dropped her to the floor and seized the book. Through her half-closed eyes, she could see him dance a little jig before he hurried to the fireplace and tossed the book on the flames.

Cynthia opened her eyes and rubbed her throat as tongues of flame wrapped themselves around Squire Manderville's special book. The flames pried open the pages and blackened them in moments. Cynthia reached out for the knife lying next to her and quickly put it under her apron before Dickon looked back at her.

Tears were in his eyes.

"We are not free of him. I burned the book, but we are not free."

Dickon faced the fire and sobbed as Cynthia rose to her feet. Her brother had tried to kill her and had burned the stolen book. They only stole the book to get money for passage to America, and the daft fool had burned it instead.

She stepped close to him.

He had tried to kill her, his own sister. And now he sobbed over the book, his pale, fat neck shaking.

Cynthia raised the knife and plunged it into his flesh. She wrenched it out and struck again and again. The blood surprised her as she struck a fourth blow.

Dickon fell to the floor. She watched him writhe and felt sorry for the brother she knew, not Dickon, but someone else a world away.

Boots pounded up the stairs, and two men burst into the room. The tall, elegant Squire Manderville struck the bloodied knife out of her hand with his walking stick and then prodded her chin up with its silver head.

"Ah, you've rid me of Dickon, sweet Cynthia, but your petty rebellion will still be punished well enough."

He was looking at her as he spoke, but his gaze seemed fixed above her eyes, as if he spoke to someone taller, more polished, more Hollywood than she. Squire Manderville then stepped aside, revealing his partner at cards. She briefly recognized the man as Mr. Morozov, looking decidedly sheepish in Eighteenth Century britches.

"Take her," Squire Manderville said. "And lock her in the tower."

Silently, Mr. Morozov bound her hands and led her into the dark.

His Queen of Darkness

"Is this interview going to be about me or Mike Vlasov?"

Anna Verdango looked at me from across her cigarette, and for an instant I thought it was 1944 and she was between takes on Dark Inheritance.

But then the smoke cleared, and I could see her wrinkles and the liver spots on her hands. Dark Inheritance had just come out on VHS, and Mike Vlasov was long dead.

"Well, I would like to write a book about Vlasov. Or at least his movies. He must have been an interesting man. He was a real artist. I mean the stuff in his movies holds on to you for days after you've seen it. Weeks."

She crushed out her cigarette.

"He was a damn Russian in love with death. He only looked profound because the people next to him were making Deanna Durbin musicals."

I shifted in my seat, and she fixed me with merciless blue eyes.

"You're right about how his crap can hold on to you. It's held on to me for years, and you're almost too far gone yourself. If you want a happy life, burn all your notes on Vlasov and forget his movies. Never see them again for as long as you live."

My mouth opened as I thought of burning the notes for my book, and she laughed, a sharp, barking sound.

"You're doomed. It's too late for you. It's too late for me." She lit another cigarette. "I'm his Queen of Darkness."

XXX

When I first saw Anna Verdango, it was 1944 for her and 1984 for me, but thanks to the magic of Mike Vlasov, it was 1774, and we were in the Transylvanian foothills.

This guy, Francois Merillion, a young French tutor, has left the civilized world to take a job with the Werdegast family. I could relate to that. I had graduated a year before with an English degree, and after a year of living in the basement typing other people's term papers, I thought maybe the only call for my talents might be in Transylvania.

Francois walks to a crossroads, where a body hangs from a gallows. A big Orthodox priest with a terrific beard is standing there praying. The tutor asks the priest about the Werdegasts. The priest keeps praying, but his unhappy eyes speak volumes. He gives Francois a look that remembers all sorts of unspeakable deeds in the past few centuries and, more important, promises more to come in the next 75 minutes.

Then this carriage storms up, forcing the tutor to step away from the priest. The camera moves in for our first look at Anna Verdango – long hair, strong eyebrows, and pale skin. Her expression, as befits Katya Werdegast, is haughty. You know she has the serfs whipped for walking too loudly. You know, even though the movie is in black-and-white, that her hair is red, the color of hellfire and damnation.

"Who are you?" she asks Francois.

When he answers, Katya leans back and smiles at him, revealing the legs of the hanged man behind her through the carriage window.

It's all there, beauty and death, desire and punishment, in the same shot.

That was when I put the remote down and knew I was going to watch <u>Dark Inheritance</u> to the very end.

XXX

"I came to Hollywood in 1939. I was on the Atlantic when Stalin signed his agreement with Hitler. I was lucky. I've always been lucky. I was in an airplane during the last earthquake. Never knew it was happening, and it was over when I landed.

"I came with Franceska. We were like sisters. She was the one Hollywood wanted, but she said, 'Not without Anna.' MGM learned I was a redhead and said I could come. I guess they were short of redheads that year.

"We came and they gave us new names. I was Nancy Meadows, and we danced in a number in <u>Broadway Melody of 1940</u>, but they cut our dance and dropped our contracts. Warners picked us up, and we danced in the saloon in <u>Virginia City</u>. I studied English every night, but Franceska went to parties and met Peter Lorre. He introduced her to John Huston. That is how she got dialogue in <u>Across the Pacific</u>. Then she went on to <u>Background to Danger</u>, <u>Mask of Dimitrios</u>, still later <u>Moulin Rouge</u>.

"Me, I was too busy studying English to meet Peter Lorre. I said, a smaller studio will have bigger parts for me. I went to Universal for <u>Spring Parade</u> with Deanna Durbin. I screamed in <u>Sherlock Holmes and the Voice of Terror</u>. Maria Montez sacrificed me to the volcano in <u>Cobra Woman</u>. Lou Costello sprayed water in my face in <u>In Society</u>. And then I met Mike Vlasov."

XXX

I let the tape recorder play her words back to me. So she was a Nancy for a while. I didn't think I should let my Nancy know that. She thinks I spend too much time on old movies in general and Mike Vlasov movies in particular. She wouldn't even sit through <u>Dark Inheritance</u>.

"It bothers me that you like stuff like that," Nancy would say. "It's about a man who's in love with a werewolf."

"He survives."

"He's sick. It's really disturbing that you identify with him."

"He's the most intelligent man in the movie."

"And he's sick. And you get up at 2:30 so you can watch that garbage at 3 AM."

"So when we buy a VCR, I'll buy the Dark Inheritance tape, and I'll watch the movie at a normal time."

But would Dark Inheritance work at a normal time? Would its images cast the same spell if the phone rang in the middle of it with Jan calling for Nancy and then chatting for a half-hour until "The End" appeared on the screen, so Nancy could hand up the phone and say: "Well, I don't see what was so special about that. It didn't hold my attention."

No, Dark Inheritance needed the 3 AM time slot. You blink yourself awake and sit in front of the only light in the house, the TV screen. You know that everyone else is asleep, everyone who thinks that English is a stupid major, everyone who knows just what you did wrong and why you'll never make it. They sleep, and you watch this werewolf movie that's really about failure. The guy who is the most intelligent person in the movie sees his crummy tutoring job end when the family gets wiped out. The woman he loves dies as well. Complete and utter failure, the last thing you'd expect to see in a Hollywood film, but Mike Vlasov got it on the screen.

You watch this movie about the persistence of old evils and curses passed on from parents to children, and you realize that all the other stuff on TV, the stuff that tells you how to change deodorants and get friends or why you have to buy the newest car is just crap. Dark Inheritance says that all roads lead to the cemetery, and after watching it you can see that all the commercials are there to distract you from that fact.

Mike Vlasov's vision of the world folds itself around you at 3 AM, if you're ready to receive it.

XXX

"You've seen photos of Vlasov, of course? They don't do justice to his eyes. Deep, dark brown Russian eyes. *Ochi chorniya.* You could lose yourself in their depths. I just had to keep looking into them.

"Why did you let them call you Nancy Meadows?' That was what he asked me. 'They didn't call Garbo Ann Smith. If they had, would she have starred in <u>Ninotchka</u>?'

"Vlasov wasn't of Universal. They'd brought him in to pep up their horror line after <u>Frankenstein Meets the Wolf Man</u>. He had left RKO in some bad odor. Maybe he had talked back to some fathead or punched someone's son-in-law in the nose.

"Going from RKO to Universal… in those days that was going downhill. At first, I thought that was why he was sad. Those eyes never smiled. He could say the funniest things – he could make Karloff laugh like a child – but the humor never reached his eyes.

"But studio politics meant nothing to him, and I heard that his family had been killed after the Revolution, just like the Tsar's. That explains his eyes, I told myself. He must have seen it from under a bed or through a closet keyhole, not daring to make a sound while the Bolsheviks killed everyone he held dear, the poor soul.

"Didn't I feel like a horse's ass then when he told me his mother had brought him over to America in 1912? He went on to make it clear that they had sailed in August of that year, and there had never been a chance they would have sailed on the <u>Titanic</u>.

"He laughed. 'I know you, Annushka,' he said. 'You think up more dramatic stories than all my writers put together.'

"So I never knew where that unmeltable sadness in his eyes came from. He never let me get that close."

There's this scene in which the Werdegasts and Francois are seated for a banquet, and the old Count, Karloff in his white powdered wig, his mouth twisted into a permanent sneer, gets into a shouting match with Francois, who announces that he can't teach the Werdegast children since their parents are so ignorant.

Katya, who wants Francois to stay, runs weeping into the night, out under the full moon, and the change begins. She looks up at the moon, mist encircling her, knowing and dreading the change to come, but also wanting it, the freedom from thinking, the freedom from arguing about aristocratic privilege and politics. The only freedom that matters from now on will be the freedom to run through the dark hills and kill the weak.

As she wants the change, her hair gets longer and longer, and her eyebrows darken and grow together. Her nose and mouth start to pull forward into a snout, and then, before she gets too ugly, the film cuts to a long shot of her on the hillside, her hair flowing down past her knees, as she falls to all fours and howls at the moon.

Nobody ever laughs. I've seen Dark Inheritance at the New Carnegie and as part of Taylorville State University's horror movie marathon, and nobody laughs. One guy tried once, but he'd been drinking, and I shut him up.

Katya runs over the hill and kills a shepherd. You never see her face until after the deed. Remorse. Shock. But you can also see she's pleased. It's like a post-coital thing.

She hurries back to the castle, and as she runs, her hair gets shorter. We know she's becoming human again.

Suddenly we see Francois, holding a torch, standing before the door. His hair is disheveled, and it sounds like he's been yelling himself hoarse for her.

Cut to Katya as he sees her. Her eyebrows are still quite dark, and her face has a wild, dangerous expression. To love such a woman means risking savage death and eternal damnation, for she is also a beast.

He looks at her, and you can tell from the play of expression on his face in the torchlight that he doesn't care about those consequences. He has fallen in love with that inner beast, perhaps because of the hint of death and damnation.

I know I did.

XXX

"The transformation scene in <u>Dark Inheritance</u>? Well, Jack Pierce was a genius. He didn't want to repeat his Wolf Man make-up, and, frankly, I didn't want to be turned into a grotesque. The three of us had a conference, Pierce, Mike and I. Pierce came up with what we used, the long hair and the eyebrows."

(A long silence follows on the tape.)

(That was the first lie I told you. Maybe I haven't said the whole truth here and there, but I haven't deceived you until now.

Mike Vlasov thought of the eyebrows and the hair. But he was smart about it. He could introduce an idea into a conversation and let someone like Pierce believe it had really been his idea all along. Pierce certainly told everyone he had come up with the look.

Yet the way Mike hung around the sketches for the makeup and the tests never let me forget he was the true father of the idea. That she-werewolf look, that meant something to him.

We became lovers. He was married, but his wife was a tiresome woman all caught up in re-electing Roosevelt and rather openly embarrassed by the type of films her husband made.

The day we filmed the transformation scene, Mike came to the set with Karloff. They presented me with a cake. Boris was all smiles, glad to see someone else run up long hours in Pierce's torture chair for once. Mike hovered in the background and let Bob Klug direct the film. Still, I knew those haunted brown eyes never missed a thing I did while I wore that makeup. I could tell what he wanted, and I thought I could finally melt his sadness.

Bob pronounced himself satisfied with the day's work, and Pierce was ready to remove my make-up. Just then word came from another set that Junior was throwing a fit on the Mummy movie, and Pierce had to hurry off to calm the bandaged star.

I had just picked up Variety *to kill some time when Mike entered the dressing room. Guilt was all over his face, and I knew that Junior's fit wasn't an accident. I'm sure a case of scotch changed hands sometime.*

His eyes were never sadder than when he knelt by me in the torture chair. As if he were the one surrendering. I almost made a joke and said he should play Francois, but no sooner had I thought of it than I knew it would wound him if I did.

I kissed him then, in my makeup. I took his hand and put it on my breast. Events soon took their course.

That was the last time we made love.)

XXX

There's good stuff here, but I think she's holding something back. She talked about how wonderful and sharp Vlasov was up to about the middle of filming Dark Inheritance, but from then on she only talked about Bob Klug or Karloff or even Jack Pierce and how sweet and wonderful they were and how much fun they all had.

It's like she doesn't walk to talk about Vlasov after a certain point.

Maybe they were lovers, and she doesn't want to tell me.

I think about Anna and how she was when she filmed Dark Inheritance and what it would be like to see that red hair and pale skin in real life. I wouldn't blame Mike Vlasov at bit if he had tried a fling with her. I mean in that Look magazine "Pharaoh of Fear" article, his wife said that it would take a tank to drag her to one of her husband's movies. There's a comment that can really put a strain in a marriage.

Actually, Mrs. Vlasov sounds a lot like Nancy. Hell, the last time I tried to watch Dark Inheritance on AMC, she called it that same old boring black-and-white shit.

I hate that, and I hate how she sighs when my book comes up. It isn't a big waste of time. It's my way to get out of my rut and change things. Plenty of people will want to read about Mike Vlasov.

When the book comes out, maybe we could put a picture of Anna on the cover, in her Dark Inheritance makeup. I know I couldn't resist that if I saw it.

"I guess I did better by changing my name back to Anna Verdango. Dark Inheritance played nearly 5 weeks at the Rialto in New York. Still, it was the only film I made with Vlasov. After they saw me in that, Universal cast me as the murder victim in The Black Angel. Dan Duryea was such a nice man, even if he did strangle me.

"Did I ever see Mike Vlasov again after Dark Inheritance? Not really. He was doomed when Universal became Universal-International. The new management went highbrow and wanted to phase out horror movies. Vlasov would have been a natural for film noir. He could easily have produced The Killers or Criss Cross, but the U-I management knew best, and they knew he could only make werewolf movies. So they kept him in what today you would call 'development hell,' and that's where he was when he died."

XXX

"So what do you want to talk about today?" she asked as I set up my tape recorder on the restaurant table. "My television career? The Man from U.N.C.L.E.?"

"I'd like more about Dark Inheritance."

"It's only a movie, not the secrets of the universe." She lit a cigarette. "You take too much interest in that film."

"It's a good one."

"The Black Angel is hardly bad. The Far Country is good too, although it was damn cold to film. Do you want to hear my Jimmy Stewart story?"

"They don't speak to me like Dark Inheritance does."

Anna Verdango laughed.

"And what does Dark Inheritance say to you other than 'This is a Universal production'?"

"You're making fun of me."

Anna raised her hands. "I am sorry, but I can't believe that someone born after that movie came out should find it so fascinating."

I sighed, and I hoped that I wouldn't sound stupid.

"Well, maybe I just saw it at the right time in my life. I was in the same situation as Francois, trying to find the right path in life. Of course, he found a grand, dark adventure, falling in love with a werewolf. Me, I just went on typing other people's term papers. Then I got a job typing mailing lists."

"Your life is your fingers," she said.

I looked at my hands. "And I'm not even a concert pianist."

She laughed.

"I decided to write a book about Mike Vlasov's films as a way to break out," I said. "So I came to California like Francois went to Transylvania."

She exhaled a stream of smoke and put a wrinkled hand on her chest.

"To meet me," Anna said. "But, sadly, I'm not really a werewolf."

"No," I said. She wasn't a werewolf, just a nice older lady who had been in a movie I liked way too much. I knew there wouldn't be any great revelation from her this morning. Sitting here, across from her, I realized that asking her if she had been Mike Vlasov's lover would be as disgusting as asking my grandmother if she had been Herbert Hoover's mistress.

"I really ought to get to the airport." I stood up. "I have to change planes in Chicago."

"Good luck," she said.

Anna crushed out her cigarette and stood up. She offered me her hand to kiss. "I hope the book helps you, Francois."

The "Francois" threw me for a moment. Then I realized that this was the star of <u>Dark Inheritance</u> standing close to me.

"I'll miss you, Katya," I said and put my arms around her.

We kissed.

XXX

"Annushka," the young man said in a voice I hadn't heard in decades. "Annushka, how lovely to see you."

I stepped back and sat down suddenly, my eyes wide with terror. That voice had been stilled for decades. When the young man reached out and took my hand, I nearly screamed.

"How alive you are," he said. Two sad brown eyes now looked out from his face. With his left hand, he touched his upper lip and laughed. "It's been so long since I had a moustache. I suppose it's the style now."

"What… what did you do to that boy?" I asked once I was sure that I wouldn't scream.

"He is…" He shrugged. "Elsewhere. He may even be enjoying himself. He knows so much about <u>Dark Inheritance</u> that it would have been cruel not to send him there."

"What? How?"

Both his hands gripped my right hand, and his brown eyes bored into mine.

"How? I can't say. What? It seems I collect souls. They come to me via my old movies, the ones Deborah wouldn't see unless she were chained to a tank." The young man's face suddenly creased with anger lines suited to the face of man more than twice his age. "I…" He struggled for the right words. "My art seems to have this power."

Those eyes, so sad, looked past me. "The first ones I took were my enemies. The others were those who scorned me. Speak no ill of the dead, Annushka."

He closed his eyes and shrugged. "But I tire of their fears, their agony, their stupidity. I am the only one who knows. Alone."

His hands gripped mine tighter, and I knew what he would ask.

XXX

I released Anna as the wind blasted my face. A chill gripped me, and the sound of water splashing over rock puzzled me. I hadn't noticed a fountain in the Old Vienna before. I looked down to see that I was standing on a bridge over a stream of water racing down from the hills. Over Anna's shoulder I could see the castle of the Werdegasts. Anna herself was suddenly free of wrinkles. Incredibly young and lovely, she regarded me with warmth and admiration, just as she regarded Francois is <u>Dark Inheritance</u>.

Just as.

"Francois, take me from here, away from this fog of superstition and tower of ignorance. I know that there is no Werdegast curse, only a sickness in my mind. When we are out of sight of these mountains and that dreadful castle…"

"You will never leave these mountains."

As I turned to look, I knew I would see Boris Karloff striding to the bridge. The wind unfurled his cloak behind him, and he jabbed the ground with the end of his sliver-headed walking stick with each step he took.

This was no actor playing a role, I told myself. This is a maddened nobleman determined to keep his daughter under his thumb.

Murder in his eyes, he stopped and pointed at the moon with the head of his stick.

"It is the Werdegast blood, Katya, that enslaves you to the moon, that calls you forth to kill, that will still flow through your heart whether you flee to Paris or not. You will never be free of the curse. Never escape its power."

Like a puppet, I felt myself be moved to stand between father and daughter, to act the movie hero, even though with each second I found myself thinking of them more as Count Werdegast and Katya than Karloff and Anna.

"Let us go," I said, as I walked to the edge of the bridge. My voice sounded flat and unconvincing in my ears. "Your day is finished, Count Werdegast. Everywhere mankind is breaking the chains of the dark past."

Those might have been the words of Francois Merillion pouring out of my mouth, but the voice remained stubbornly mine, utterly without French accent or much inflection or conviction. For a moment, I hoped a director would yell "Cut!" and demand an actor who knew how to deliver a line to step forward and take my place.

But there was no director, no camera, and no microphone. This was real.

Gripping his walking stick like he intended to use it as a weapon, Count Werdegast took a step closer and declared: "Shut your mouth, Frenchman. You'll never take Katya away as long as I draw breath."

I knew my lines and my movements.

"Titled fool! You'll not see the sunrise. Look!" I pointed to my right. "Your serfs are rising to destroy your cursed home."

With an animal-fast turn of his head, the Count glanced away to see the torches of revolt flicker on the hills. But then he turned his furious gaze to me. Roaring, he charged, and barely raised my arm in time to take the blow of that silver orb.

Pain shot through my left arm, and with my right hand I grabbed his stick and tried to wrest it out of the old maniac's hand.

"Never be free!"

From behind me, I heard Katya snarl, and I knew her final transformation had begun. My heart sank as I knew I would never see her as a normal woman again, except in the peace of death.

That is, if I didn't die first in this version of the movie.

The Count jerked his stick back, and the movement swept me off my feet, and I let go and fell to my knees. I gasped, marveling at the old man's vigor.

He roared, and I leaned aside. The blow that might have cracked my skull landed on my shoulder. The Count pulled the walking stick back and with a laugh jammed its head into my solar plexus.

All my breath whooshed out of me, and I tumbled backwards, rolling down to the stream. I could barely manage to grab a breath before I plunged into the icy water that swept me under the bridge. Frantic, I clawed against the stream, trying to swim to the castle bank, when my side slammed against a rock. I swallowed a mouthful of water and spat it out, my nose burning. I turned and grabbed the rock, heaving myself out of the water. I blinked like a newborn, trying to see what had happened.

Katya had transformed. Her long hair flowed down her back. The Count stood wide-eyed with terror, blood streaking the sliver head of his stick. On the other side of the bridge, torch-wielding peasants stared in horror.

"Never be free!"

The werewolf's howl answered the Count's defiance.

XXX

"I am alone, Annushka. I need you. I…" The brown eyes seemed lost in so young a face. My hands felt crushed in his grip.

"To live in your black-and-white horrors? To be a monster, turning into a werewolf so you can have me as a lover?" I snorted. "Did you like me better as a woman or as a beast? Answer me that."

"Annushka, I was ashamed of myself ever afterward." He closed his eyes and released my hands. "I loved you, and I wanted the beast I had created, and I hated myself for making you that beast."

I turned away from him and picked up my cigarettes and lighter. I looked at my wrinkled white hands as I lit up.

"You would be as you were then," he said. "Your hair would be red, not gray. Your skin would be unwrinkled, as timeless as the image in a film."

He put his hands on my shoulders and kissed my neck.

"You would be my Queen of Darkness, to help me rule my kingdom of shadows."

I drew on the cigarette and turned away from him. To be young again, safe from old age and death, I thought. It would be like being in an airplane during an earthquake.

I had always been lucky after all.

I exhaled and turned to face him.

"What about the boy? Will you set him free?"

He nodded.

"As my queen wishes."

Yes, I thought. I had always been his queen of darkness.

XXX

Everybody told me that she didn't suffer, but I still felt guilty, like it was my book that made Anna Verdango drop dead in the middle of the Old Vienna.

I thought about her a lot on the flight back and while waiting between planes in Phoenix.

No matter what I remembered, I told myself, I couldn't have been in Dark Inheritance. That kind of thing just doesn't happen to people.

Nancy met me at the airport when my flight got in. She asked about my trip. I told her it was fine, and she just started telling me about her brother breaking up with his new girlfriend and going back to his old girlfriend, and I had to admit that it felt much less real that those black-and-white images that engulfed me for those moments when Anna Verdango had a seizure and died.

I lugged my suitcases and listened to Nancy talk about the merry-go-round of relationships. After a while, my mind started to drift.

For the last scene of Dark Inheritance, after Katya's death, Francois staggers past the now-empty gallows. He's leaving

Transylvania, and his face shows that he'll always be haunted by what he saw there. Some words are superimposed on the image of him walking against the wind, past the empty gallows. They say something predictably pat and liberal about Enlightenment and darkness, but I never paid attention to that.

I always tried to read Francois' expression.

Those words always seemed the phoniest part of <u>Dark Inheritance</u>, and I suspected that Mike Vlasov let the studio put them there because from the look on Francois' face any alert viewer knows that the young Frenchman, for the first time in the movie, doesn't know what to think after his dark adventure.

My dark adventure now.

The black panther's mouth stretched wide open, the shocking whiteness of its teeth and the dark pink of its mouth causing Alice to take a step back even before the beast's cry reached her ears. It sounded like a scream, like someone falling under a railroad train as the locomotive whistled, but it was just the panther crying as it looked at Alice, its green eyes meeting hers.

"Forget it, Sam. This is a bad idea," Alice said, raising her voice so she could be heard over the brassy version of "After the Ball" that blared from the merry-go-round and all the other noise that spilled from the Maumee Carnival.

The two of them stood off the carnival's midway, in front of a red wagon trimmed with gold paint. Alice, tall and brunette, looked down at Sam, who kept his eyes on the iron bars of the panther's cage. At the top of the bars hung a white sign with red letters that proclaimed "MIDNIGHT the black panther from Borneo."

Sam's right hand closed on Alice's shoulder and gave her a shake.

"None of that, Shoogey. It's a great idea. A photo of you standing by Midnight. That 'Beauty and the Beast' stuff is always a winner."

Sam's hand slid underneath Alice's long black hair, and his fingertips touched her neck. He gave her a little rub as he stood there, grinning.

"I saw this beauty, and I had to think of you right away. It's a natural, don't you think?"

Alice looked at Midnight, who had started to prowl around the cage. The big cat didn't look like he took any grief from anybody, yet there he was in a cage. Sam was always telling her now mean she looked, and yet here she was, with him still managing her career. Maybe, Alice thought, Sam did have a point about her being like Midnight.

"Look at that beaut," Sam said. "All that black hair. That danger. You get yourself dolled up in a black gown, your hair done just so, and you look pretty dangerous too. We get that on a photo with Midnight in the background looking over your shoulder, and clubs can put that up on a board outside, and they'll have to beat the suckers off with a stick."

Alice shook her head, and Sam lost his grip on her neck. She dug into her purse for her cigarettes and laughed as she fished them out.

"Beauty and the Beast, huh? If you bill it like that, some wise guy's going to ask which is which."

The black panther stalked back and forth behind the iron bars of its cage. Its eyes always watched Alice as its powerful shoulders moved back and forth. Alice put a cigarette in her mouth and looked at the beast until the panther's back-and-forth started to make her dizzy. She switched to looking at the bars, which didn't move. Thankfully, they looked very thick.

Sam slapped her on the back and laughed.

"What a kidder." He waved a finger at her. "That crack tells me you like the idea. It's good. We'll build you up as a woman of mystery. Do you think you could do that thing, you know, have your hair hang over one eye?"

"No." She struck a match and lit up.

"That's what the people want, you know. The only thing that makes Veronica Lake a star is her hair. But you've got hair and a voice."

Alice blew smoke at him. "Thanks."

Sam clapped his hands together. "I'll get Marty and his camera over here for some test shots. I think he was by the hot dogs when we left him. He never misses a chance to feed his face." He motioned her to go over to the cage. "Go make friends with your new co-star."

Alice watched him retreat back into the carnival crowd. The merry-go-round now played "Roll Out the Barrel." As Sam walked away, the panther let out another cry, and Alice turned to face it. This time, the panther stood looking straight at her, and she could see a long and narrow red line on the beast's right flank. The panther raised its head and gave out a long wail, making Alice think again of sirens and tears.

She dropped her cigarette to the ground, stepped on it, then got out her compact and inspected herself. Her green eyes stared back at her from the mirror, and she had to look at the panther again.

"There is something about the eyes," she said to herself. She shivered and decided to touch up her lipstick.

"Here by yourself, doll?"

A tall muscular man in white pants and a white T-shirt, cigarette tucked behind his left ear, smiled as he walked up to her. He flexed his muscles to show off the snake tattooed on his right arm, then he tipped an imaginary hat to her. He pointed toward Midnight's cage.

"Just here at the carnival with your sister?"

Alice didn't say anything but capped her lipstick and took out another cigarette.

"Friendly sort, ain't you? Too good to talk to people?"

"My friends will be right back," Alice said, and waved back to the midway. "Why don't you go buy some popcorn?"

"A fella's got a right to stand where he wants, don't he? And I want to stand right here." Smiling, he walked up to Alice and reached out for her elbow.

She blew smoke at him. "Go someplace where you're

wanted."

"You know, your claws ain't as sharp as your big sister's there. You should be more polite to people."

He grabbed her by the left elbow, and Alice jammed the cigarette into his hand, between the thumb and forefinger.

The panther roared as the man cried out. He yanked his injured hand back and gave Alice a backhanded slap with his left hand. She stumbled back, and he stepped closer to her.

"That wasn't friendly at all. Here I was having a nice little talk with you, and you had to do that."

The panther snarled again.

The man looked at Midnight. "Shut up!" He looked around and saw a bottle lying on the ground. He grabbed it, smacked it against the wagon's wheel, and broke off its bottom, leaving nice sharp brown shards sticking up.

"C'mere, kitty-kitty," the man said, stepping closer to the bars of the cage.

Alice watched as he gestured with the broken bottle. A black paw swung out through the bars, and, laughing, the man struck at it with the bottle. A high-pitched cry burst from the panther, and the man shouted in triumph. Alice could see blood on the broken glass.

"Want more?" the man said, turning his weapon back and forth in front of the panther's face. "I'll give you more."

He took a step closer to the bars, and Alice ran into him, slamming both her hands into the small of his back and shoving him.

Yelling, the man stumbled forward against the bars of the cage, his face pressed between two of them, as the beast sprang.

XXX

Alice looked up at the ceiling and tried not to hear the

screaming and the off-key "Strawberry Blonde" that kept playing whenever she tried to fall asleep.

She sat up and lit a cigarette. Closing her eyes brought the whole thing back. The jerk's wailing as Midnight tore into his face and slashed his shoulders. The crowd of popcorn eaters and hot dog chewers running over from the midway. The cop blowing his whistle like he was going to swallow it, pulling his gun and taking three shots to put Midnight down.

Alice looked at the burning tip of her cigarette. Nobody had seen her push the jerk into the bars. They just assumed she was another gawker out for a look at the blood. The old guy with the huge white moustache who had owned Midnight just kept crying and crying like the cop had shot his wife or something.

"Midnight! Midnight!" The geezer had almost made it sound like there were three syllables in it.

Sam took it nearly as hard. He had found Alice and just hung on to her arm as she steered him out of the carnival.

"It was a natural," he kept saying. "Beauty and the Beast. I knew it was a natural as soon as I saw her."

Alice crushed the cigarette out in the ashtray. Nobody had seemed too choked up about the dead guy, a carny roustabout who didn't seem to have any friends.

"As if I can talk," Alice said. Apart from Sam, she guessed, there wasn't anyone who really cared if she lived or died.

Alice threw herself back on the bed, took a deep sigh and watched the lights from the all-night movie house across the street flash across the ceiling. Maybe, she thought, she should have gone to the show. Watching Bette Davis get sick and die might make her feel better, but she doubted it.

The light spilled across the ceiling, then vanished, letting the darkness leap back, only to drive it out again for the moment. Back and forth, back and forth went the play of light and shadow, and after a bit, Alice could feel herself beginning to relax. She wasn't holding her neck so tight, and the pillow felt good as she nestled her head against it.

Again and again, the light and the shadow changed places above her. Alice's eyelids drifted shut, only to jerk open as the light rushed across the ceiling. But after a heartbeat, her eyelids began to close once more, and Alice felt so tired.

She realized that the light didn't totally go away when the darkness came back. Above her were two little islands of light that stayed in the same place even though the rest of the ceiling was pitch black. She wondered how they could do that, stay there, even when the light from outside was off momentarily.

The two specks became annoying. They didn't make sense. They should be dark like the rest of the ceiling, Alice thought. Were they getting larger?

Alice's mouth opened, as if to ask a question, but it closed because Alice realized there wasn't anyone here to ask.

The little lights were getting bigger, she realized. She squirmed in her bed, uncomfortable at this unexplained thing. They were about the size of eyes, and she felt like she was being watched. She wanted to get up and leave the room, but her legs didn't obey her.

They were green, the eyes. When the light from the theater slashed across the darkness, Alice now could see the two green eyes very clearly. She tried turning her head away from them, but her neck wouldn't let her.

Now below the eyes, something new was taking shape on the ceiling. It looked like a stain, a large stain. Alice raised her arms, and they flopped around but refused to grab the sides of the bed and help her get out. She willed her eyes to close, but that tired her, and her eyes opened again. Alice gave a short gasp.

The stain had resolved itself into a mouth, an open red mouth that stood out against the blackness that surrounded it every other heartbeat. Alice blinked, but the image stayed above her. The darkness around the eyes and the mouth now seemed thicker than the shadows that appeared when the light retreated.

Tears welled up in Alice's eyes as she looked up. It had become a face now, one that she recognized. The black panther's head loomed above her, mouth open in a silent roar, eyes blazing in pain.

Alice tried to twist her head away from the vision overhead. Her neck ached as she tried to move to the right, to the left, but no matter how much she hurt, she could not get away from the face of Midnight, which grew ever larger.

Wetness fell from the panther's eyes, striking Alice in the face. She reached for her face, to wipe the beast's tears away, but something seized her arms and forced them to the bed, as the silent crying continued, and Midnight's tears ran down Alice's cheeks and into her mouth.

Suddenly, the beast itself was above her, claws, paws, shoulders and tail. It sprang from above and hurled itself at her. Alice screamed as the panther slammed against her chest and entered her heart.

She sat bolt upright and tore at her pajamas, trying to seize the beast. She couldn't grab it, so she ran the backs of her hands across her face, trying to wipe away the animal's tears. But her cheeks were dry.

Alice sat there, letting the light from the movie marquee flash on and off. She blinked. Slowly, she turned, putting her feet on the floor.

"Nightmare," she said.

She got up and walked over to the window. The theater marquee continued to flash DARK VICTORY at her.

A short laugh escaped her.

"Maybe Bette Davis will put me to sleep," she said.

In a minute Alice had gotten dressed and was out the door. She skipped the elevator and hurried down the stairs. At the edge of the lobby, she paused until she heard the gentle snore of the night man, his head pressed forward against the detective magazine he'd been reading. Silently, Alice strode across the lobby, pushed the revolving door, and stepped out into the night.

She paused outside the hotel, letting the door turn behind her until it stopped. To her left she could see several couples in line at the movie theater, but Alice now found her attention pulled away from its flashing lights. She looked down the street to her right and noticed a small sign saying "Pat's" over a beer joint several doors away on the same side of the street as the theater. Somewhat surprised, she began walking along the sidewalk away from the big marquee, toward the small sign, feeling as if a chain were attached to her throat.

She slowed her pace as the door to Pat's opened, and three men stepped out on the sidewalk. Two of the men were clearly friends, and one kept his arm around the other's shoulder as they walked toward the movie theater and traffic light. The third man, shoulders slumped, walked in the opposite direction.

Alice ran across the street to Pat's once the two men had gone a distance. Her eyes never left the back of the tired man walking in front of her. She shot a glance through the window into the bar. The bartender was talking to a bald man who was very agitated and kept jabbing at a newspaper with his finger. No one was looking out at the street, and Alice rushed past the bar's door.

As she got closer to the slow man, he looked more and more familiar to her. He turned his head to look for traffic before crossing E. 35th, and as she pressed herself against the bars of a jeweler's shop she recognized his white moustache. Her movement rattled the bars a bit, but the man took no notice.

He walked across the empty street and started to whistle as he moved along the waist-high stonewall that ran along the edge of the Granger Cemetery. His shoes scraped the pavement, and he put a hand on the stonewall to steady himself.

Alice pushed herself away from the bars and charged across the street. She ran faster than she had ever ran in her life, bounding across the dark pavement at her prey. Her mouth stretched wide as she charged her prey. The man turned, and the fear that wafted from his every pore spurred her on.

Her forelimbs struck the pavement, and she hurled herself forward as he tried to boost himself over the wall. She leaped and her paw came down on his neck as he collapsed against the stone.

As the old man struggled, Alice raised her head to the night sky and cried out, a shriek that the bartender at Pat's would later describe as sounding like a train whistle.

"What do the cards say?" Andrew asked, his intense pale blue eyes looking across the dimly lit table at Julia as the band on stage suddenly quieted, letting the bald trumpeter begin his solo.

Julia quickly lit a cigarette and turned away from Andrew. The whiteness of the cigarette contrasted with her brown fingers as she took a deep drag. She'd never seen the cards say anything like this before.

The trumpeter played a slow, mournful tune, and the white couples on the dance floor gripped each other more tightly and slowly turned this way and that, dreaming of tropical beaches and cloudless blue skies.

Julia's hand trembled, and she inhaled deeply again. Her eyes closed, and her face creased in a frown. She shook her head and exhaled, then willed her face to look pleasant before she turned back to the blond man sitting across the table from her. She beamed at him and reached for the cards.

"I'll shuffle again. Mr. Victor wouldn't like me to read bad fortunes."

Andrew reached out and grabbed her hand before she could touch the cards.

"They'll only come out the same way again unless you cheat. I don't want you to take that risk. I'm not a tourist, Julia. I'm Andrew. Just tell me what the cards mean. I need to know."

Julia pulled her hand free and took another deep drag on her cigarette. Blinking rapidly, she crushed it out in the ashtray and looked down at the cards again, hoping against hope that they had changed.

They hadn't.

"You will marry a corpse." Her voice broke on the last word, and she sounded as if she would cry. "And--"

The blond man held up his hand before she could say more. "It's the cards, not you. I know that. I know that you wish me well, despite everything."

"Andrew." Julia shook her head and pointed at the cards on the table. "I see strong magic. The deadliest magic."

"Strong magic." A note of anger crept into his voice. "Strong magic that Cynthia and my mother should never have played around with. But they did." He looked at his watch. "I ought to get back to Dark Cypress now."

"I'll come along."

Andrew smiled, and Julia remembered how handsome he could be. "You have a job here. I don't think Mr. Victor will keep you on if you leave now."

"The devil with Mr. Victor."

Andrew scowled again. "The devil with my mother. And Cynthia. Look, Julia, I'm no knight in shining armor. I'm too weak for that... for what you want me to be." He looked away from her. "For what I want us to be. I can't fight a hundred-fifty years of Kenworth tradition."

He stood up abruptly, skidding his chair back so fast that it fell over just as the trumpet player's melody was reaching for a crescendo. The gunshot-like sound broke the musician's concentration, and suddenly the dancers looked around and started to grumble.

"Goodbye, Julia," Andrew told her. "Read the cards for yourself. I'm sure you'll meet a dark handsome stranger someday."

He walked to the exit, oblivious to the stares of the patrons as the trumpet player began his wailing ascent again. Julia lit another cigarette and saw Mr. Victor striding across the floor at her.

"You dumb jungle bunny, I told you to tell no bad fortunes.

What the hell did you say to him?" He raised his hand as if to strike her, but Julia simply dragged on her cigarette. Mr. Victor turned and looked at the patrons, smiled and lowered his hand. He leaned close to Julia.

"Wasn't that Andrew Kenmore? Don't you know how much pull his family has in this county? He could make a lot of trouble for us."

"You'll never see him again," Julia said. She blew a twin jet of smoke. "And you'll never see me again either."

She stood up and ran toward the back exit, leaving Mr. Victor flummoxed, caught between trying not to make a scene and not wanting to let anyone, especially a woman like her, have the last word with him. Seeing her rush out into the night, he reached down and swept her cards onto the floor with a contemptuous gesture.

Outside, Julia looked around, her eyes getting used to the darkness. An old cab sat near the exit, its driver reading the newspaper.

She rapped on his window.

"Take me to Dark Cypress."

The pudgy driver blinked at her in surprise.

"Sugar, you know I'm just supposed to take the band back to the hotel."

"They're still playing, and they've got three songs left." She opened her purse. "Just take me to the bridge, and I'll give you an extra $10. If you get in any trouble, Mr. Victor can take it out of my salary."

The driver shrugged, and Julia got in.

The moon seemed especially near and white as the cab sped to the Armstrong bridge. The moonlight outdid the streetlights and made the waves of the bay sparkle in a way Julia had never noticed before. It all looked so pretty that the fortune she had seen in the cards for Andrew seemed ridiculous, until she looked up at the moon and saw its merciless eyes staring down. Her grandmother's name for such a moon on such a night came back to Julia.

"A calling moon," Julia said to herself.

"Calling moon?" The driver shivered. "I don't want that kind of talk in my cab. None of it."

"Sorry." She looked at the pale light dancing atop the dark waves. The lights spun and smashed into each other before getting sucked down into the swirling darkness around them. Seeing the darkness triumph again and again began to depress Julia, and she closed her eyes and leaned against the window.

"You sweet on that Kenmore boy? He sure hangs around a lot if there's nothing going on. He sweet on you or something?"

Julia lit a cigarette and looked at the back of the driver's head.

"Just get me to the bridge as fast as the cops'll let you."

The driver gave a low bitter laugh. "Yes, your majesty."

Julia smoked and thought of Cynthia Armstrong. Skin as pale as a porcelain doll, with hair the color of butter, Cynthia had never let slip that she knew Julia was alive. Julia, and her pull on the affections of Andrew Kenmore, was simply something a well-brought up lady refused to mention.

Cynthia lay there like a spider in her bed at Dark Cypress, her web spreading over the whole town. At times, Julia thanked God for the horse that threw that spoiled rich girl and made her a cripple, and at other times she cursed that animal, because she knew that the accident had only given Cynthia more power. She could imagine Cynthia lying propped up on her pillows, her doll-like eyes wide and guileless, blinking back tears as she bit her lips and looked at Andrew.

"But Andrew," the spider would say, "I so want for you to be my husband." Life has dealt me such an unkind blow -- the unsaid words would swirl around his neck, knotting themselves into an unbreakable rope -- don't inflict another upon me.

"Here it is," the driver said, as the cab slammed to a halt. He stuck a huge hand back at her. "Remember my extra ten dollars."

Julia quickly put the money in his hand, and he closed his fist around it and turned away from her. She stepped out into the muggy night air and looked across the bridge to Dark Cypress. The waves crashed around the short pylons in frantic bursts of activity.

"It's a long, lonely walk," the cab driver said before Julia slammed the door. He chuckled at her through the window, then sped away.

"You will marry a corpse." The memory of her words to Andrew came back to Julia. They made no sense, but Andrew had acted as if he knew exactly what they meant, and he had come here.

Julia shook her head. Death and the whisper of death had circled Dark Cypress lately. The undertaker had been summoned across the bridge to Dark Cypress two weeks ago, yet when he got to the he had been rudely turned away by Mrs. Armstrong without even being able to step out of his hearse. Only a couple of days ago, he had come back to pick up Mrs. Armstrong's body.

All kinds of rumors and suspicions now flooded in on Julia. Cynthia Armstrong hadn't even shown herself to the undertaker when her mother's body was taken away. More worrisome, perhaps, was that no one had seen Dr. Leon for about two weeks now. His shop had been closed with an "Away until further notice" sign held in place under the skull door knocker. No matter how tight money was no one dared rob Dr. Leon's shop. Some said the sinister man had last been seen hurrying toward the Armstrong bridge the very day the undertaker had been sent packing.

Julia thought about the change in Andrew, how he had been so happy to see her the Saturday before last, as if a weight had been taken off his shoulders. Tonight, however, he had simply seemed beaten down by life.

A few lights were still on at Dark Cypress, and they offered Julia some hope that life went on as usual on the island. Andrew was out there, she told herself, and she should go to him if he were in trouble.

With a sudden caw, a bird flew overhead as if pursued. Julia shivered and realized that although it had seemed muggy when she got out of the cab, she felt a distinct chill now. She put her hand on the handrail and began walking along the metal grill walkway toward the lights of Dark Cypress.

"Andrew," she said, as if in prayer. "We'll come back from this place, Andrew."

The waves beneath the bridge slapped the metal of the pylons and their stone supports. An odd moan rose to Julia's ears as she walked. She blinked and realized that it must be the birds resting for the night underneath the bridge. From out on the bay, a freighter sounded its horn as it pulled away from the docks.

Julia's mouth was dry. What would Cynthia Armstrong say to her if she just walked in to Dark Cypress? What would she do? Julia remembered the story her mother had told the neighbors, about a woman who had gone to Dark Cypress before the last war to demand money from the Armstrongs for her child. Her body had washed up under the bridge, after the eels had had their way with her eyes.

Julia looked over her shoulder, back to the shore. She stood at the halfway point, she guessed. She forced herself to look ahead to the large house and how its pale columns shone in the moonlight. Andrew wouldn't let anything bad happen to her, Julia decided, and continued walking forward.

There hadn't been much traffic across the bridge since the undertaker had been sent away, Julia remembered as her footsteps clicked against the metal grillwork. The birds below began to coo, and some flapped their wings making sudden explosions of sound that made Julia step faster, eager to get land under her feet again.

Dark Cypress drew nearer and nearer. She thought she

could recognize Andrew's car parked out front. It was hardly more than a runabout, not like the huge Packard the Armstrongs used. Julia's mother often joked that if the Armstrongs ever ran out of money, they could rent their Packard out as a hearse.

Julia had laughed then, on the mainland and in the sunshine. Now, above the waters of the bay as a cloud passed over the moon, the joke didn't seem funny.

The bridge began to dip down to Armstrong island, and as soon as she became aware of the descent, Julia put on a burst of speed, running outright the moment she reached land. Drooping cypress trees loomed ahead of her, but beyond them she could see the lights in the windows.

"Andrew," she said.

Suddenly, she stopped. It was as if she had heard a gunshot, but nothing had disturbed the dark quiet. Julia turned to her left, and noticed a pathway leading into the cypresses, yet she hesitated to follow it, to put her feet onto its well-worn groove. Instead, she walked parallel to it, beneath the droopy boughs.

Down the path she could see the frame of a doorway that must have opened into a long-abandoned coach house. Now the moonlight showed the overgrown wreckage that lay behind the ever-opened door, the fallen tree trunk stretching across the decaying boards. Julia hardly focused on the triumph of nature. Instead, her eyes went to the shape hanging from the doorway.

A small shape, much smaller than a child, it hung with its snout pointed toward the night sky. Its fur was matted to its body, and the moonlight showed where the birds had feasted on its eyes.

Julia blinked and, after a moment, remembered a bright and clean poodle yipping at the end of a leash as Andrew walked along Market Street taking it to the veterinarian for Cynthia Armstrong.

That poodle had been the only creature Cynthia Armstrong had ever loved, and now she had had the poor beast hanged.

"What sin did you commit?" Julia asked.

A cry cut through the night. Julia nearly fell to the ground. The cry came again, and Julia thought it sounded like Andrew.

Without a thought, she overcame her earlier fear, leaped onto the path and started running toward Dark Cypress. She shoved the dog's body aside as she ran through the empty doorway and leaped over the fallen tree. She ran faster and faster toward the mansion, as fronds of cypress lashing at her face.

The path was taking her to the back of Dark Cypress, where, she could see, someone had built a big fire. A white man, hands pressed to his face, swayed back and forth on his knees. Before him stood two white women, one old and stooped, one young and unnaturally straight. Off to the side, a stout black man struggled to hide his laughter behind his massive hand but failed.

"Why did you do this?" Andrew didn't look at the women as he rocked back and forth on his knees. "Why?"

"For you, Andrew," the older woman said. "You could never be happy without Cynthia. There is no one else suitable for you to marry."

Julia reached the edge of the cypress trees and stopped. She recognized the older woman as Mrs. Kenmore, Andrew's mother. Her pale, wrinkled face beamed with joy as she walked toward her kneeling son. She held out a thin, paper-like hand and patted him on the head as he sobbed.

"I know you're overwhelmed, Andrew, but you shouldn't show so much emotion in front of the colored."

With her head she motioned toward Dr. Leon, who stopped laughing and wiped the back of his hand across his mouth. Sweat glistened across his bald head, and he grinned broadly as he looked first at Andrew and then at Cynthia Armstrong.

Cynthia stood utterly still in the firelight. Her skin seemed as ghostly white as the moonlight, and breathing did not make her chest did not rise and fall. Eyes unblinking, she looked at Andrew, her face unlined by any puzzlement at his anguish.

"Andrew," her voice sounded dry and unnatural, forced up through protesting organs. "I love you Andrew. You will always be mine, and I yours."

"Oh, God." Andrew turned away from her.

"I will never get old, Andrew," Cynthia said. "Age will never touch me. We can live here together forever. Dark Cypress will always be our home."

"You idiot!" Andrew leaped to his feet and shoved his mother back. "Was this mansion worth this blasphemy! Do you want me shackled to this corpse for all time so you can say your son is master of Dark Cypress?"

"But it's all for you, Andrew," Mrs. Kenmore said, shaking her head in puzzlement. "It's all for you."

"All for you, sonny boy." Dr. Leon laughed. "The biggest house in town and the coldest wife."

With a howl, Andrew threw himself at Dr. Leon, who stumbled back in surprise. Andrew's white hands closed around the wide black face, and he jammed his thumbs into Dr. Leon's eyes. The doctor's laughter turned into a scream as blood ran down his cheeks from his sockets.

"Andrew!" Mrs. Kenmore's hands fluttered.

Roaring, Andrew turned and yanked Dr. Leon toward the fire. The chubby man tripped over his feet and fell screaming headlong into the blaze. His arms sent burning logs and embers flying as they swung back and forth.

Julia screamed. Andrew, his face twisted with rage, turned to her. He blinked rapidly, raised his bloodstained hands, then looked away.

Dr. Leon heaved himself up from the fire, flames now

sweeping around his jacket He beat at his face with his swollen hands and ran blindly toward Dark Cypress. Mrs. Kenmore gasped.

"Stop him. Stop him, Andrew! You must. He'll ruin Dark Cypress."

Andrew raised his gory hands but did not touch his face. His shoulders shook as he looked at Julia. He smiled as the sound of breaking glass reached him.

"My wedding night. My mother is so proud of me. I am to be master of Dark Cypress. Her life's ambition is realized."

He pointed at the broken window where Dr. Leon's body had set the curtains on fire. Flames had raced up to the ceiling and smoke had begun to spill into the night sky.

"The grandest house on the bay, and it will all be ashes by morning. But I'll be in Hell before then."

"Don't talk that way, Andrew." Mrs. Kenmore was wringing her hands together ever faster. Suddenly, she noticed Julia and frowned. "You don't belong here." She ran over to Andrew and pulled his sleeve. "Don't talk to her, Andrew. Send her away. Save Dark Cypress. You must."

Andrew turned back to Julia. "Let it burn. It was never my dream."

With a whimper, Mrs. Kenmore looked at the blazing room. "The portraits. The General's memoirs."

She trotted toward the mansion, to the French doors, as flames raced up the curtains. She raised her hands to her cheeks, then yanked the doors open and hurried into the blaze. Julia could see her rush to a massive desk and start tugging at its drawers, as smoke billowed past her.

Nauseated, Julia looked away from Dark Cypress, back to Andrew. He seemed tired and about to cave in upon himself. He motioned for her to go..

"Tell them whatever they'll believe," he said, gesturing to the mainland. He squared his shoulders, then walked over to Cynthia and gently took her hand in his. "My wedding night lies before me."

"Andrew..."

His face contorted in a bitter scowl and he nearly spat at her. "Go away, Julia. Go back to the living."

He threw his arms around the unmoved Cynthia, then seized the back of her head and forced her deathly pale face to his for a kiss. Julia gasped as she watched. Andrew pulled his lips away from Cynthia's and looked as if he would be ill.

"Save yourself," he said to Julia.

"My dearest Andrew," Cynthia said, in a dry, halting voice. "My love for you will never end."

"My..." Andrew turned from Julia to Cynthia. "My dearest bride."

He swept her up into his arms, and began to carry her away from the blaze that was consuming Dark Cypress. He carried his undead wife toward the calling moon, into the marsh that no amount of improvement had ever managed to drain. Julia wept and watched as Cynthia's stiff arm clung to Andrew's neck, and that gorgeous blonde hair spilled down, nearer and nearer to the dark water and muck, until Andrew's knees buckled and he fell forward, and the darkness engulfed the last master and mistress of Dark Cypress.

Dread

"I can't believe he's dead," Laura said, wringing her hands as she paced around the dining room table. She looked up toward the room where her father had been.

Dr. Whitmore's hand slipped, and the neck of the bottle clattered against the glass, spilling whiskey across his hand and onto the table.

"I said he was dead, did I not? I signed the paper testifying to his death." The doctor scowled as he looked at the spillage, then he set the bottle down and began to mop the liquid up with his handkerchief. "Don't you trust my competence as a doctor?"

"Oh, don't be angry with me, Randolph," Laura said. "There's no one I trust more about anything." She gripped the back of a chair to stop her hands. "It's just that he was always so imposing. It's hard for me to think that he... all that... is gone."

Dr. Whitmore threw his handkerchief onto the table and went over to embrace her. She sobbed onto his shoulder.

"He is all gone, Laura, and his tyranny is as dead as the Corsican's. As dead as Cromwell's for that matter. As dead as Caesar's. No longer will you be living under his thumb, unable to experience happiness."

"Oh, Randolph."

Laura looked at the doctor and kissed him. Dr. Whitmore's eyes widened in surprise, and he stepped back from her.

"Really, my dear. We must..."

The thought died as he heard a noise from the doorway,

turned and found himself looking into the enraged face of a tall, blonde woman with a sharp chin and pinched, unsmiling lips.

"I seem to have come at the wrong time," the newcomer said. "I thought that Dr. Whitmore still had duties at the asylum."

Laura, blinking rapidly, turned to face the intruder and seemed to lose an inch or two in stature.

"Ellen. How good that you came. My father would be.."

"Now that your father is dead, Laura, do you really want Miss Harkness to have the run of your house?" Dr. Whitmore asked.

"Does she really want the doctor who failed to save her father's life to have the run of her house?" Ellen Harkness asked. "But then, she doesn't seem that bereaved by his passing. And it was very convenient that you signed the death certificate."

Randolph Whitmore blinked and took a deep breath.

"Dr. Trumbull died in his sleep last night. He did not breathe this morning, did not respond to his name being shouted, and never blinked his eyes when I examined him. I have no doubt that he is dead."

Miss Harkness shrugged.

"The wish is father to the thought, as the French say."

Running his fingers through his hair, Whitmore strode forward to confront her, annoyed that he had to look up at her face.

"I am a doctor, a colleague of the deceased."

"And Horace made it clear to me that he considered you the least of the faculty, with sentimental and naive attitudes toward the inmates." Miss Harkness looked at Laura now. "He certainly would not have approved of your kissing this man, and I know that he would never consent to your marrying him as long as he lived."

"But he lives no more," Laura said, a look of surprise on her face. "He is dead, and I am free to follow my heart in this matter."

Miss Harkness opened her mouth but could not speak.

"Kindly leave this house, Miss Harkness, and never return." Laura took a step forward. "It would pain me to make the nature of my father's relationship with you public, but I would not hesitate to do so if you come back to this house."

Whitmore gasped and then applauded.

"Bravo, Laura."

A red flush came to Miss Harkness' cheeks, and she closed her mouth as her nostrils flared. She regarded Laura with a look of utter hatred, then turned on her heel and strode to the doorway. She turned again to face them.

"You shall have no happiness, either of you. I know that you did away with Horace. There is a Providence that sees such matters and avenges, and I will not rest until your evil deed is punished."

Miss Harkness scowled at the end of her speech, then let herself out into the windy afternoon. No sooner did the door slam, than Laura again threw her arms around Whitmore and kissed him.

"There is no evil deed to be punished, Randolph. We are free of her iron gaze forever."

Randolph smiled, but his eyes s trayed toward the door and avoided Laura's adoring look.

"No evil deed," he said softly.

XXX

Miss Harkness seized the brass doorknocker and struck the undertaker's door with three loud blows. She paused for barely three heartbeats, and then repeated her actions.

A male voice growled from the other side of the door, which only led Miss Hawkins to strike the door three more times.

The door opened just as Miss Hawkins was reaching for the knocker for another set of knocks.

"What!" The bald, middle-aged man glared as he looked out the door, realized he was looking at a lady, and then tried to smile. "Good afternoon, my good woman. How may I be of service?"

"You are an undertaker?"

The smile faded from the man's face.

"That is what the sign over my door says. Yes, I am an undertaker, Silas Greene by name, the provider of assistance to the bereaved."

"You've been drinking."

A positive scowl shaped Silas Greene's lips, and he put his arm to the door jamb.

"My good woman, I asked if I could be of service to you. If I cannot, then I suggest you be on your way."

"Was the body of Dr. Horace Trumbull delivered here this afternoon?"

The undertaker blinked, and his mouth assumed a more neutral expression, although his eyes remained unfriendly.

"That it was. May I ask what it has to do with you?"

"Dr. Trumbull had a morbid fear of catalepsy." Miss Harkness looked at the undertaker for a sign of understanding. "He feared that he might be buried alive."

"I am well aware of the meaning of catalepsy, my good woman."

"I have reason to believe that the doctor who signed the death certificate was unaware of Dr. Trumbull's fears about the condition and provided only the most perfunctory examination. I would like to see Dr. Trumbull's body."

Silas Greene regarded Miss Harkness and chewed the inside of his cheek.

"And after you see the body, you will go away, I trust?"

"Most assuredly."

Mr. Greene removed his hand from the door jamb and gestured for Miss Harkness to enter his place of business.

"I won't ask you for your coat and hat, my good woman, since you will not be staying long."

He led her into his shop, to the back, and then lit a candle to lead her down to the basement.

"You have been drinking," she said.

"My good woman, let the one who must deal with the end of life for his daily bread have a little enjoyment in this life," Mr. Greene said.

Miss Harkness sniffed. The undertaker shrugged, handed her a lit candle, and then opened the door to the basement.

The two descended the dark stairway into the cool air below.

"I have seen many a dead man," Mr. Greene said as he reached the basement floor. "And I am most certain that Dr. Trumbull was among their number."

"I will only be sure when I see for myself."

"The sentiment of St. Thomas, I believe," Mr. Greene said, as he selected a screwdriver from a table. He walked over to a plain wooden casket. "We will bury him in something much finer, I assure you."

"Something much more expensive, no doubt," Miss Harkness said.

Mr. Greene set his candle on top of the casket and walked

over to the screw at the top right of the casket.

"Have you given any thought to your burial arrangements?"

XXX

As Whitmore lit the oil lamp, Laura walked around the dark living room, rubbing her hands over her arms as if she were chilled.

"Never again will he be in this house. Never again will he sit in that chair."

She pointed at it, a vast, overstuffed armchair by the fireplace. Then she laughed, looked embarrassed and stopped.

"It almost sounds like that dreadful poem he liked to read. 'Nevermore, nevermore.' He would read it each night. I had to listen to it. I would beg him to read something else, anything else, but he would laugh and tell me it was the greatest poem written on this continent. Then he would read it, his voice sounding different, sounding like one who had seen the other shore."

Whitmore took her by the hand.

"And that's where he is, Laura. On that other shore from which no traveler returns. You need not fear him again. Ever again."

He kissed her, and she relaxed.

"Randolph," she said.

Three sharp raps came from the front door, accompanied by a woman's shouting.

"What the devil?" Whitmore asked.

"Don't answer it!"

Whitmore looked at Laura, who had gone pale. The rapping at the door came back, and he turned to answer it. Laura grabbed him.

"Don't open that door. If you love me, don't open it."

"Laura, that woman is making a scene."

Whitmore broke away from Laura and walked to the door. He opened it and stepped back as Ellen Harkness, bleeding from a long gash on her face, hurried inside from the darkness.

"He's gone mad. He's insane."

Whitmore shut the door.

"Calm yourself. Who has gone mad? Do they need me at the asylum?"

Miss Harkness stood still and looked at Dr. Whitmore with pity and dismay, and he found himself wanting to strike her.

"Dr. Trumbull has gone mad." She stepped closer to him and laughed mirthlessly. "You buried him alive, Dr. Whitman, and now he wants you to pay for your mistake, if mistake it was."

"What are you saying?" Laura walked up to Miss Harkness and seized her hands. "What are you saying about my father?"

The tall woman looked down at Laura and frowned.

"The doctor you love so much declared your father dead and tried to have him buried alive."

"Laura!" Dr. Whitmore tried to step closer to Laura, but Miss Harkness moved whenever Laura tried to turn her head so the young woman could not see him.

"Perhaps this was mere stupidity, but I did not trust his verdict and went to the undertakers to see the body for myself. When the casket was opened, Dr. Trumbull seized Mr. Greene and strangled him."

"Dear God," Laura said.

Miss Harkness gave her a pitying look and continued.

"I fled the building, but he came to my home. His mind is quite turned by grief. I do not think he can speak or understand speech. I tried to reason with him," she motioned to the wound on her face, "and you see the unhappy result."

The sound of a fist banging on the front door echoed through the hallway. Dr. Whitmore started and grabbed Laura's hand to pull her away from the door.

"You led him to us," he said to Miss Harkness.

She laughed. "It is his own house, Dr. Whitmore. He has more right to be here than you."

"Horace!" Dr. Whitmore shouted as he stepped closer to the door. "It was a mistake. An accident. I swear it was. Nothing more."

The pounding at the door stopped. Dr. Whitmore took a deep breath and released Laura's hand. He took another step to the door.

"Not dead." The words sounded as if they had been dragged across sandpaper.

Dr. Whitmore's eyes widened, and he stepped to the pane of glass to the right of the door jamb. He looked at the tall figure on the porch.

Dr. Trumbull's hair had gone white, and his left eye opened wider than his right. The whole right side of his face seemed as if it were pulled down, so his mouth seemed unable to open fully on that side. He raised his right hand to strike at the door again, and Dr. Whitmore could see that his fingernails were all broken and bloody, with cuts and scratches running along his fingers and the back of his hand.

Dr. Trumbull's left eye focused on Dr. Whitmore's face, and his hand shot toward the window pane.

Glass shattered as the hand smashed through the barrier and those dreadful fingers reached for Dr. Whitmore.

"Never bury me!"

Dr. Whitmore hurried back from the clutching hand, and ran into the small table in the hallway, upsetting it and sending the water pitcher to the floor, where it shattered as Laura screamed.

"Never bury me!"

As if infuriated by the screaming, the bloody hand grabbed for the key and turned it in the lock. Then it grabbed the brass knob and turned it, letting the door glide open to reveal the owner of the house.

"It was a mistake, an honest mistake." Once more Dr. Whitmore approached the tall, disheveled man. He held up his hands. "This can all be put right. Please let me give you something to calm you down."

A bitter grin spread across Dr. Trumbull's face.

"Whitmore wanted you out of the way, so he could marry Laura," Miss Harkness said as she ran forward. "It was no accident."

Whitmore, his face contorted by fear, turned to the tall woman.

"Keep your mouth shut. I need --"

Dr. Trumbull charged and seized Dr. Whitmore around the neck. He slammed the shorter man against the wall. Whitmore pulled at Trumbull's arms and kicked back at the older man's shins. Dr. Trumbull continued to hold on.

"Never bury me."

Laura ran up to him and seized the sleeve of his jacket.

"Father, stop. Let him live."

Dr. Trumbull took his eyes off Whitmore and stared down at his daughter. He snarled, pulling back his lips to reveal his yellowed teeth, shoved Whitmore back, and struck Laura with a backhanded blow across her cheek.

She fell to the floor, and he loomed over her.

"She's as guilty as he is, Horace," Miss Harkness said, as she pressed herself against the wall. "The two of them did it. They wanted you dead."

Dr. Whitmore ran into the living room over to the fireplace. He grabbed the poker and charged back to the hallway, arriving just as Dr. Trumbull pulled his daughter to her feet, her hair entwined around his fingers.

Dr. Whitmore gripped the poker in both hands and prepared to strike.

"Behind you, Horace!"

Dr. Trumbull turned and the poker slammed into his jaw. He flung Laura to the ground and snarled as he staggered closer to Whitmore, who raised the poker. Dr. Trumbull grabbed the metal bar and yanked it out of the shorter man's hands.

"No, no."

Dr. Trumbull pressed the metal bar across Dr. Whitmore's throat and thrust him back against the wall. Whitmore's hands scratched uselessly against Dr. Trumbull's jacket as the taller man pressed harder and harder against the shorter man's throat.

Finally, Dr. Trumbull stopped. He took a step back and pulled the poker away from Dr. Whitmore, whose body slid to the floor. Dr. Trumbull dropped the poker and began to stagger to the living room. Miss Harkness stepped close to him and took his hand.

"Your chair is here, Horace."

Laura, weeping, got to her feet and watched the two of them as they walked to the overstuffed armchair. Her father's knees wobbled as he reached the chair, and Miss Harkness hurried to ease him down to the seat before he fell.

"My love," she said.

Dr. Trumbull moaned as his legs bent, and he sat down heavily in the chair. He looked up at Miss Harkness, who leaned forward and began stroking his hair. His mouth moved as he tried to speak, but no words came out. Instead he closed his eyes and pressed his head against her hand.

A grim frown fixed itself on Laura's lips, and she moved along the wall, watching the two all the while, until she stood next to the table with the oil lamp. Miss Harkness never raised her face to see what Laura was up to. Instead, she kept stroking Dr. Trumbull's hair and murmured endearments to him.

Laura reached down and turned up the lamp to as brightly as it would burn. Then she grabbed it by its base and heaved it up over her head. Still Miss Harkness didn't look at her, and her father sat with his eyes closed, the picture of contentment.

Laura yelled as she hurled the lamp forward at her two tormentors. It shattered on the floor at the feet of Miss Harkness, and flames raced onto her dark petticoats.

Only now, as Laura ran for the hallway, did Miss Harkness turn away from Dr. Trumbull and see her. A heartbeat later, Miss Harkness looked down at the flames that were climbing her, and she screamed.

Dr. Trumbull opened his eyes. Blue and merciless, they followed Laura as she ran out of the room. He tried to push himself to his feet, but Miss Harkness fell atop him, and the chair caught fire.

Laura ran down the hallway, past the lifeless body of Dr. Whitmore. She passed him without a glance and hurried out the open door into the night. Pausing on the porch, she looked up at the crescent moon and the bright stars. The wind blew her hair, and she turned away from it to find herself looking back into the house.

The room now blazed brightly, and Laura turned away from its brightness. She took the door handle in her hand and pulled the door shut with a bang. A determined look on her face, she turned and walked across the porch, down the walk to the street that led away from her father's house.

The lantern shone its light on the unlocked chain. The guard, a fiftyish man stuffed into his uniform, stroked his chin as he regarded the chain. Wordlessly, he pushed the metal bars of the gate open and turned his lantern to cast light into the darkness.

RADLOVA ZOO read the sign that the light revealed.

The ticket booth sat empty. No one walked on the pebbled pathway. Beyond, he could see the pagoda-style roof of the Tiger House. The guard continued moving his lantern in the darkness. A massive statue of a gorilla now appeared in the light, and the lantern shook.

The guard laughed, rubbed the back of his neck, and reached down for his keys. They hung on his belt next to his pistol.

He pulled the gate shut, snaked the chain around the bars, and locked it. He pulled on the lock, nodded, and then walked off into the darkness.

As he passed the stone gorilla, he gave it a sloppy salute. Soon he passed into the darkness and was lost from sight.

Almost at once, a woman stepped out from behind the ticket booth. She wore a black cloak. Only her face, pale and smooth, could be seen in the night. She turned her face toward the Tiger House. Her eyes did not blink as she stared into the darkness, and then she began to walk, slowly, rhythmically, toward the exotic structure.

She wore no shoes. Her feet pressed against the pebbles, but she did not speed up or hesitate at all. Carefully, deliberately, her feet moved forward, step by step, toward the tigers.

A large birdcage stood to the right of her. As she passed, a long-tailed parrot flapped its wings and screamed. The woman turned her head so suddenly that the cloak fell off her head, revealing her short black hair and a scar over her left eyebrow.

The parrot settled itself back on a branch, and the woman resumed her walk. The pathway brought her to a wooden bridge that spanned the crocodile exhibit. She did not look down as she walked over the planks. Below her, the long, moonlit reptiles lay motionless. At the crest of the bridge, the woman stopped, reached up to her throat, and undid the cloak's clasp. The cloak slid off her shoulders, revealing a pale white dress.

Reaching the other side of the crocodile exhibit, the woman reached into the handbag she carried and removed a small, shiny gun. She let her handbag fall to the pathway, and, ignoring it, continued to walk toward the tigers.

One of the beasts roared, soon followed by the second one. The tigers were in large cages of wrought iron on the corners of the pagoda-like structure. Despite the unexpected noise, the woman did not stop at all.

The tiger waited for her. Its paws looked as if they had been carved from rock. The beast's ears flattened against its head, and it roared again.

The woman approached the cage. She raised the pistol, its barrel pointing up, and looked at the tiger, her eyes trying to drink in every detail of its white and tan and black fur.

Again the tiger roared. Slowly, the woman turned the gun, bringing the barrel up until it pointed at her temple.

"Hey!"

The guard rushed out of the darkness at her. The woman didn't look at him. Instead, her knees bent, and she collapsed to the pebbled pathway, letting the gun fall from her hands.

"Dear God!" The guard ran to her and turned her head to and fro, checking to see where she had had shot herself.

He put a whistle to his mouth and shrieked out an alarm. As the sound died away, he began patting the woman's face.

"It's all right, dearie. It's all right, dearie," he said.

He realized that he had not heard the tiger in all this commotion. The guard turned and looked at the great beast, who lay with his eyes closed on the floor of the cage.

XXX

"It was Oskar's most exciting night in his twenty years as night watchman," Dr. Viktor Korlevski said. He smiled, as he took in his brother's look of absolute attention, then sipped his coffee. "You remember Oskar, of course."

"The devil take Oskar," Dr. Milos Korlevski said. "Who is this woman who attempted to kill herself in your zoo?"

Viktor glanced at his wife, Mira, and Milos' wife, Elizabeth. Both women sat stiffly in their places and wore frosty expressions. Again, Viktor allowed himself a smile.

"There is quite a story about that. She had been coming to the zoo every day for a week." He put a spoon in his coffee and stirred it. "She would only go to the Tiger Pavilion, where she would watch Rustam as he padded across the floor. Back and forth the great beast would go, and she would simply stand with her back against the far wall, watching that orange-and-black behemoth stalking imaginary prey. She took that spot so she could see the entirety of his cage without moving her head. She stood there, unblinking, day after day, in a kind of trance, I would imagine."

"In God's name, why?" Milos asked.

Viktor allowed himself the smallest smile, then raised the coffee cup to his lips and took a sip. He was a middle-aged man, with graying hair and a clean-shaven face that glistened with perspiration. His clear blue eyes looked out at the world from behind glasses.

"I think the answer to such a question more properly lies in the realm of your study than mine, brother." He raised his hands briefly. "I deal with the animal kingdom, with simple beasts that hunger and act upon their hunger."

Dr. Viktor Korlevski dabbed at his mouth with his napkin and then continued.

"You, Milos, plunge into a jungle more terrifying than any found near the equator. You presume to explore the realms of the human mind. How many more dangers could befall an unwary explorer in that shadowy kingdom than in the Amazon or Congo?"

"Ah." Dr. Milos Korlevski balled up his napkin and then flung it down into his lap again. he turned to his wife Elizabeth.

"You hear him? You hear how he insults me while sounding like he compliments me? The constant struggle of the older brother to maintain dominance. No doubt lions and great apes behave in this fashion, and I am sure Viktor has memorized all their lessons and tricks."

Elizabeth, a blonde with a heart-shaped face, began to laugh, but raised her hand to her mouth and turned the noise into a cough. Across the table, Mira Korlevski glared at her and glanced over to her husband, Viktor.

"As you would say, dear Milos, in olden times, such a person as this Natalia Dorda would have been burned at the stake for witchcraft." Viktor allowed himself a sympathetic look, and then put the tips of his fingers together. "The mystery of why a modern woman should be so obsessed with jungle beasts is something, I think, that your science of psychology should unravel fairly easily."

Milos snorted as his brother leaned back in his chair.

"And having delivered himself of his challenge, the king gorilla rests and waits for his unsuccessful challenger to slink away into the foliage." He chuckled. "Viktor, as you said, you are my older brother. I have been studying you all my life, and you fail to understand how utterly predictable you are."

Milos slapped his hand against the table, making a sound like a gunshot. Mira gasped and dropped her fork. Dr. Milos Korlevski stood up.

"Give me a month," he said. "Thirty days. I will get to the bottom of this matter by the end of that time."

"Never," Viktor said.

"Name a wager, if you are so certain of my limits."

"Your limits and the humbuggery of your field."

"Name a wager," Dr. Milos Korlevski said.

"A thousand kronas and a half-page in the <u>Radlova Tribune</u> admitting failure." Viktor's eyes held no mercy. "The winner shall write the newspaper piece by himself, and the loser has to pay to publish it."

Dr. Milos Korlevski extended his hand.

"Accepted."

Dr. Viktor Korlevski grabbed his brother's hand and shook it.

"It shall be a pleasure seeing you fail."

XXX

Dr. Milos Korlevski opened a folder on his desk, dipped his pen into the inkwell, and looked up.

"What is your name, please?" he asked.

"Natalia Dorda," the dark-haired woman said.

She wore a brown dress with a simple scooped neck that did not reveal much of her bosom. Her attention drifted to the window and the bars over it.

"You are a secretary?" Dr. Korlevski asked.

"As if that is the most interesting thing about me," Natalia said, turning her attention to him. "May I smoke, please?"

"If it will help you answer my questions."

"I work as a secretary at Bruckner's. I am thirty years old. I am divorced, and I have no children. My mother is my only living relative, but we have not spoken in several years."

Dr. Korlevski put down his pen. "You spoke that with the enthusiasm of a student reciting the life of Julius Caesar. You give the impression that these are meaningless facts about a person who died long ago."

"May I smoke?" Her eyes were intense and unblinking.

Dr. Korlevski's finger tapped against the paper.

"Will it make you more forthcoming?"

"I can hardly be less forthcoming."

With a chuckle, Dr. Korlevski raised his hand as if in blessing.

"You may smoke, then."

"Thank you."

Soon smoke swirled around the woman's short black hair as she thought.

"Natalia Dorda… is someone who died to me long ago, seven years in fact," Natalia Dorda said.

"You seem quite alive for one who died."

"Natalia Dorda was a good woman who loved her husband and wished for children," Natalia said. "Unfortunately, her husband came back from the army a drunk and unable to hold a job." She rubbed her left cheek. "When I took steps to save myself from going down with him, family and friends turned their back on me."

She took a puff and then looked at the burning end of her cigarette.

"Everything Natalia believed in turned out to be false. It all let her down." She shrugged. "It was then my dreams began."

"Dreams?"

"There is my real life, and there are my dreams." She chuckled. "When I am awake, I ride the streetcar, I show up for work, I type and file, I go home, I cook. But when I sleep, I go where I will. Those who cross me fear my wrath and flee before me."

Natalia began to smile.

"I am not mousy little Natalia. No. I am different."

"Who are you then?" Dr. Korlevski leaned forward. "What are you then?"

"My grandmother told me a tale her grandmother told her," Natalia said. "A village girl once went into the woods to find a veshaya."

Dr. Korlevski suppressed a smile.

"Her man had wronged her." Natalia took a last puff on her cigarette. "The priest had told her to stay with this man, but she went to the veshaya instead."

Natalia crushed out the cigarette.

"The veshaya made her walk on all fours," Natalia said. "She killed her worthless man, and the villagers chased her through the woods and killed her. They cut off her hide and burned it, but they never walked boldly in the darkness after that. For still she walked the night."

"Have you met a veshaya?"

Again, Natalia's cold, dark eyes glared at the doctor.

"It was a grandmother's tale," she said. "Nothing more. I know that. But I dream."

She looked at the far wall and fell silent for a long moment.

"I walk through the woods, and it is different. I do not walk on two legs in my dream. I look for people, but not for companionship. I have companionship with no one in the dream," Natalia said.

She took a deep breath.

"A grim existence, then." Dr. Korlevski underlined something.

"In my dream, I look for people in order to kill them." She ran her hand through her hair.

"It frightens me." Natalia looked at Dr. Korlevski, blinking rapidly. She trembled. "I do not want to stay in the woods. I want to be with people. To be accepted by them. I do." She looked at her shoes. "But I cannot."

Dr. Korlevski put his pen down.

"This is why you have not been to your work for the last week?"

Natalia nodded.

"And why you tried to kill yourself the other night?"'
Natalia closed her eyes.

"I want to stop myself," she said. "I want this to stop."

"This?"

"This loneliness! This pain!" She pressed her face into her hands.

"Do what you must to end this. Any test. Any experiment. I... I can't go on like this."

"Is everything to your liking?" Dr. Viktor Korlevski asked.

The laboratory was in the Zoo's research building, where the animals were measured and studied, and newborns were taken care of.

"The conditions are quite satisfactory," Dr. Milos Korlevski said.

"The last patient to use this room was a redhead," Viktor said. "A Bornean orangutan. Not anywhere near as lethal as the one of Herr Poe's imagination." He walked over to the third story window and glanced down on the roof of the Reptile House. "But then I always find Poe makes most of an impression on me when I have been drinking too much strazhvik."

Milos regarded his brother with a bland expression.

"You will not get me flustered before the session, dear brother," he said. "I understand your jealousy. I can guarantee that you will be astonished at what psychiatry will achieve in this century. The best days of zoology, on the other hand, lie in the past."

"There are 21 days remaining in our bet," Viktor said, smoothing his moustache. "Just so we understand each other."

"Of course." Milos walked to the door and opened it.

"Please have Miss Dorda sent in."

Milos closed the door and walked over to a chair and table that faced a blank wall. He examined the syringe that lay on the table, and then waved at the two booths that had been set up opposite the blank wall. He nodded when his signal was returned.

"Douglas Fairbanks tonight?" Viktor asked.

"All shall become clear to you very quickly," his brother said.

The door opened, and two nurses, one male and one female, escorted Natalia Dorda into the laboratory. The male nurse was thick and muscular. The female held Natalia's hand and smiled at her.

"Please bring her to this chair," Milos said. He smiled at Natalia. "And how are you this evening, Miss Dorda?"

She did not answer him at first. Her gaze swept around the room, and she noticed the booths and the syringe.

"I feel as if I shall be performing in a play," she said. "I'm so excited."

"This is only the beginning," Milos said. "In any event, you will be sleeping through the experiment tonight, and every night."

"Sleeping?"

"You will be hypnotized," Milos said, taking her hand and easing her into her seat. He motioned to the female nurse to ready Natalia's arm. "You won't remember a thing, but what you might tell us in such a state would be invaluable to our knowledge."

Natalia looked at Milos. Her eyes were warm and blue.

"Cure my loneliness," she said.

After the nurse swabbed down Natalia's left arm, Dr. Milos Korlevski injected her with the serum. Then he straightened himself and told the male nurse to turn down the lights. As the nurse walked across the room, Milos raised his hand and motioned to the two booths.

At once, mechanical noises leaped to life, and a circle of bright light appeared on the opposite wall. As Natalia tried to focus her eyes, the number 100 appeared briefly in the center of the circle. It flickered out, and then 99 appeared.

Soon Natalia began counting backwards. After 55, she began skipping the even numbers, as she was speaking so slowly though she wanted to keep pace.

Dr. Milos Korlevski picked up a notebook and pen and wrote the date.

"Who are you?" he asked.

"I am…." Her voice faded out in uncertainty.

"Who are you?"

"Gli… Glizelka," Natalia said. "I am Glizelka."

"And where are you, Glizelka?"

She laughed. "The woods. The woods beyond my village."

From against the side wall, Dr. Viktor Korlevski watched, his eyes wide.

"Why are you in the woods?"

"They hate me." Her words were quiet, yet there was iron behind them. "They hate me, and they wish I were dead."

XXX

The great orange beast stretched and shook as it walked out of the shadows.

A familiar odor, a mix of blood, anger, bitterness, called to her, and so the great orange beast stepped along the alley to the back door of the apartment building.

The odor carried memories for the great orange beast. An angry face, an open mouth, white hair.

"You're unnatural."

The words echoed again and again in the beast's brain.

Someone had left a brick to keep the back door propped open. The beast raised a paw and pushed the door back, then leaped into the darkness.

"You're unnatural." The words appeared before her like white letters cut into blackness.

The great orange beast followed the odor. She scrambled up the back staircase, three stairs at a time, her stripes rippling along her back as she climbed.

The first floor went by. The second and third followed quickly. With every step, the odor became more intense, more irresistible, more annoying.

"You're unnatural. You're no daughter of mine."

The fourth-floor blazed past.

And then she stood on the landing of the fifth floor.

Her tail twitched as she breathed in the odor, its hate, its betrayal, its judgment.

The great orange beast lowered her head and made a rumbling sound in her throat.

Then she began to walk, deliberately, along the fifth floor, past the janitor's closet, past two apartments, past the elevator.

Each step took her closer to the apartment she knew. The apartment she had gone for many holidays.

The apartment where she had been cursed.

"Unnatural. No daughter of mine. Get out!"

She stood outside the door and raised a paw. It slid down the wood, scratching four deep lines in its trail. Again she raised her paw and scratched the door.

"What the hell is this?" a woman's voice came from within. "You evil children! I'll tell your parents, you worthless imps!"

The door swung open, and the old, angry woman stood there.

Her eyes widened, and she stepped back. Her mouth moved, but she could not speak.

The great orange beast walked into the room. It looked into the eyes of its mother.

Its prey.

Back and back again, the old woman retreated before the great orange beast.

The beast opened its mouth and roared. The noise let the woman scream at last. She shut her eyes, slammed her hands over her ears, turned away from the beast, and ran.

The glass of the window shattered, and suddenly the screaming stopped.

XXX

Dr. Viktor Korlevski shook his head as he glanced through the notes he had taken. Then he took another sip of coffee and looked across the restaurant table at his brother.

"You have material here for a fine macabre tale," he said. "One worthy of Morozek or Conan Doyle. But I don't think you are getting any closer to a solution to the mystery that is Natalia Dorda."

"It was so kind of you to refuse to suspend our wager while she dealt with the aftermath of her mother's death," Dr. Milos Korlevski said.

"If you had wanted that flexibility in the wager, you should have specified when we made the agreement." Viktor's face became all seriousness.

"Look, this is clearly a case of hereditary insanity. The woman's mother throws herself out a window. Who knows how crazy she had been? It is an unfortunate certainty that Miss Dorda inherited her suicidal impulses from her mother."

Milos sighed, then dabbed the corners of his mouth with his napkin.

"There is a difference between leaping from one's apartment window and shooting oneself in a public place. And if this were a mere matter of inheritance, why should this suicidal condition turn up in the daughter before the mother?" He shook his finger at his brother. "Victor, you simply are wrong."

"You're whistling in the graveyard, dear brother. You are going to lose this wager, and you know it."

Milos threw his napkin into the bowl of ice cream.

"I have arranged to hypnotize Miss Dorda again tonight. You will be there, I trust."

"Nothing could keep me away," his brother said.

XXX

The door to the laboratory opened, and a male and a female nurse escorted Natalia Dorda into the room.

"The movie that puts me to sleep," she said as she looked around the lab. She gave a half-smile. "Why do you hate the Kino so much, Dr. Korlevski?"

"I don't hate the Kino at all," Milos said. "I think it has done much to educate the public about the ideas of psychology."

Dr. Viktor Korlevski, standing by the wall, laughed.

Natalia gave Viktor a bitter glance, then turned back to his brother.

"I too enjoy the Kino. It is an escape from the self, is it not?"

"Possibly." Milos motioned for her to sit in the chair. "Please."

Natalia laughed.

"Suddenly the proper doctor is in charge," she said. "Was my comment about escaping from the self too close?"

"We are all servants of time," Milos said.

"I think it was," Natalia said. "Who would you escape from, Dr. Korlevski? Is there a Mrs. Korlevski at home?"

"Please be seated. We need to get started as soon as possible."

"There is," Viktor said. "And she is quite formidable too, I can assure you."

Milos clapped his hands. "I must insist that we behave like adults. Panina Dobra, please seat yourself at once."

Wordlessly, Natalia took her position in the chair. Dr. Milos Korlevski injected her, and the movie began.

XXX

"Thank God the rain has stopped," Mira Korlevski said, as she and her sister-in-law stepped out from the theater.

The street and sidewalks were wet and glistening thanks to the neon lights above. The dark-haired Mira wore a long, black coat. The blonde Elizabeth sported a shorter coat with a collar lined with fox fur.

Thunder rumbled overhead.

Mira looked up.

"It could let go any time, and then we'd be drenched."

"If you're so worried," Elizabeth said. "Hail a taxi."

"These modern dramatists," Mira said, glaring back at the hall. "Tricking people into paying good money to watch squalid trash. Getting caught in a storm would be just the icing on the cake for a wretched evening like this."

"Just get a taxi, Mira. You can sermonize on the ride home."

Scowling, Mira ran toward the curb. She reached the edge and raised her hand, just as a blue taxi squealed over to attend to the man just behind Mira. Water leaped up from the gutter and soaked Mira from the hip down.

"Ah! Ah!" Her arm shook with rage and she walked back to Elizabeth, who struggled not to laugh.

"Take that coat off," Elizabeth said. "You can have mine for the night."

"This has been the worst night of my life," Mira said, as she unbuttoned her long coat.

"I'll go hail a taxi," Elizabeth said. The two women exchanged coats. Mira put on the coat with the fox trim, while Elizabeth hung the wet coat over her arm.

"Elizabeth?" a man said.

"Who..." Elizabeth looked at him. "Good heavens! Jiri!"

The young man threw his arms around Elizabeth and pounded her back.

"I didn't know you were in Radlova!" Elizabeth said.

"My semester ended, and I still had money left," Jiri said. "So I decided to come into Radlova and see the play that everyone's talking about."

"What a waste of money," Mira said.

"Mira, this is my cousin, Jiri," Elizabeth said. "My sister-in-law."

The two nodded at each other.

"I haven't wasted all my money yet," Jiri said to the women. "I was thinking of going to Gureniak's and having a sandwich. I'd love to catch up on old times with you, Elizabeth. It's been nearly a year, hasn't it?"

"It certainly has." She smiled at him. "How grown up you look!"

Elizabeth turned to Mira.

"I'm going to hail a taxi and go home and get into something dry," Mira said. "I would only be a third wheel on such a happy bicycle anyway." She nodded at Jiri. "Enjoy the last of your money in Radlova."

"Thank you," he said.

"Are you sure?" Elizabeth asked.

"Yes, yes." Mira walked away from the two.

She looked at the line of taxies in front of the theater and sighed. Thunder rumbled again, and she glanced up at the clouds. She grabbed the fur collar and pulled it tight around her neck before hurrying off toward the next block.

She glanced down the service alley as she crossed it, not entirely noticing a dull orange shape that stretched and stirred as she walked past.

Several couples waited for taxies along this block as well. Mira sighed and kept walking. The theater and its lights now lay behind her. Fewer lights cut into the darkness on this block. Mira found herself slowing down, as if unwilling to give herself over to the dark.

A taxi pulled away, leaving a vacant spot on the sidewalk, beneath a streetlight. Mira ran toward the pool of light. Her hand shot into the air.

"Taxi! Taxi!"

She looked to her left. No one waited on this side of the block. She turned to her right. A short man with a red face and a white moustache stood on the edge of the curb, on tiptoe, glancing about as if he might summon a taxi by sheer will power.

Mira laughed at his earnestness.

And then she heard something, a breath, but a deep breath, as if something large were nearby. A chill ran up her spine, and gooseflesh spread across her shoulders. Something scraped on the pavement that made her think of sharpening a knife on a whetstone.

Her mouth went dry. She wanted to turn and look in the direction of the sound, and she was desperately afraid to. Her heart beat faster, and she opened her mouth as if to scream, but she held it in.

A blue taxi pulled up in front of the short man, who pulled open the back door and got in.

Mira wanted to call out, to ask if she could ride to, to ask if he could see the thing in the darkness so near to them, but her voice caught in the dryness, and the taxi sped away.

The thing behind her breathed again.

She ran, and as she moved, the silence in her throat shattered, and her screams burst forth into the night air. People standing on the other block suddenly turned their heads to see what was going on. To see why this woman screamed…

To see the taxi slam into her.

XXX

"Tonight is the last night," Viktor said as he watched Milos adjust the chair for the third time in five minutes. "You have heard plenty of details about grandmother stories and half-forgotten sensationalistic novels, but you are no nearer to finding out why this woman wanted to shoot herself outside the tiger house."

"There is still tonight," Milos said. "She reached the end of the tale about Glizelka. That means she can't hide herself behind that character any more. She will have to reveal the truth."

"The truth!" Viktor raised his hand and made a sweeping gesture. "The truth is not in what people say, but in what they do. The truth is that Mira ran out into traffic. Did that dismal play upset her so much? Did she think that someone was chasing her? What difference does it make? The truth is that she ran in front of a taxi and is dead."

Milos lowered his eyes.

"If you want to delay these tests," he said, "until a time when you are more interested..."

"No. It shall be tonight, as we agreed." Viktor's face was red. "Why should I go back to an empty house and brood? Better to stay here and see you fail." He pointed at the screen. "This is all just nonsense, trash and lies leading to more trash and lies. You had thirty days to find the truth. You will fail tonight."

Milos bit his lips and stood silent for a moment. Then he relaxed, ran his knuckle over his mouth and walked over to the door.

"You may send her in," he told the male nurse.

Viktor walked back to his usual spot on the side. He shook his head.

"Another night of meaningless chatter," he said. "But it will be worth it if it teaches you a lesson about the folly of your profession."

Moments later, the two nurses led Natalia Dorda into the laboratory. She walked with confidence and paid attention only to Milos.

"You said last time that you believe tonight you will find what has tormented me," she said. "It made me happy."

"I hope to find a solution," Milos said, turning away from her to look at his clipboard.

"Dr. Korlevski," Natalia said. She raised her hand. "I know that you are married, but forgive me, I wish it were not so. You have been so kind to me…"

Viktor laughed from against the wall.

"Well done, Milos. You have made a conquest. You have failed to accomplish your scientific goal, but you have won the heart of this silly woman."

Natalia's face turned red. She lowered her hand and looked away from Milos.

"Thank you for caring about me, Dr. Korlevski," she said.

Milos led her over to the chair, and she sat down. Before he could step away, Natalia grabbed his hand.

"I loved you," she said. "Remember that."

The female nurse made ready Natalia's arm, and Milos gave her the injection. He signaled for the movie to begin, and Natalia leaned back in her seat and watched the screen.

"One hundred," she said. "Ninety-nine. Ninety-eight."

By the time she said "Ninety," the film was well into the eighties. Her jaw moved slowly, and her eyes glazed over.

"I'm sorry," she said as the numbers marched on. Her head dipped forward.

Milos stepped closer to her.

"Can you hear me?" he asked.

There was no response.

"Can you hear me?"

This time, she seemed to move her head.

"Can you tell me where you are?"

Again, the black-haired woman's head moved. A noise, a moan, started in her throat.

"Where are you?" Milos asked.

The moaning became louder, and her downturned head began to shake from side to side. Milos put his hand on her shoulder, and the woman suddenly sat up, throwing her head back.

She screamed.

An instant later, glass shattered. A huge orange tiger burst through the laboratory's window, and shards of glass flew everywhere.

Viktor Korlevski cursed and began pulling glass from his face when the great beast leaped at him. Before he could move, the tiger's jaws closed on his left elbow.

"Natalia!"

Milos reached for her, and seized her shoulders, but her head hung forward, and she did nothing when he shook her.

"Doctor!" The female nurse grabbed Milos' arm. "We must escape!"

Milos and the nurse ran to the door as Viktor screamed. Milos pulled it open, and let the nurse run into the hallway. He followed, but as he pulled the door shut, the tiger ran at him and got a paw in front of the door. It batted the door back.

Milos and the nurse ran in different directions. She ran to the left toward the elevator, while he turned right for the stairs.

The tiger bounded out into the hallway and turned to the right.

Milos rushed down the stairs three at a time. From behind him, he could hear the roaring of the tiger, and he fought the temptation to look back.

"The tiger is loose! The tiger is loose!" The nurse screamed from a window.

Milos' foot slipped on the final landing, and he swung his arms like a windmill so as not to fall. Again the tiger roared, and Milos ran toward the doors of the research building. He charged into the door and felt it burst open before him. His momentum took him out, only to trip over an uneven slab of concrete, and he fell to his knees.

The tiger roared louder than ever.

Three gunshots rang out, and the roaring stopped.

Milos looked up at the startled figure of Oskar. The stout night watchman, his face bright pink with amazement, held his pistol with both hands.

Only now did Milos look over his shoulder at the crumpled orange beast behind him. The animal's right forepaw quivered for a moment, and then it became still. The beast seemed less impressive by far now, even smaller.

Milos pushed himself to his feet, and he wiped the dirt from his knees, then ran his fingers through his hair before turning to the night watchman.

"Bravo, Oskar! Buffalo Bill himself couldn't have done better."

XXX

Oskar stepped into the laboratory, followed at once by Dr. Milos Korlevski. Oskar shook his head and put his pistol back in its holster, while the psychiatrist walked over to the chair and the woman who sat in it.

She sat upright, with her eyes closed. A bloodstain above her heart marred her dress.

"Dearest Natalia," Milos said, as he put his hand on her shoulder. "How can you forgive me?"

Threatening purple clouds moved east across the late afternoon sky as the stagecoach rolled past the forest. Francois Merillion looked out the window at the clouds and frowned. He consulted his pocket watch and closed it with a look of dismay. Leaning back against his seat, he began to whistle.

"Please, don't whistle," his fellow passenger, a merchant, said. He raised a finger, and Francois noticed his thick fur cap. "To whistle indoors means to whistle away one's money."

Francois kept a straight face, except for his left eyebrow, which rose slightly.

"Really," he said. "I had never heard that. This part of the world has such unusual beliefs and customs."

The merchant snorted.

"I can tell you don't care for our ways, but we didn't invite you here, after all."

Francois tipped his tricorn hat at the merchant.

"In fact, one of you did invite me to this corner of the Empire. Count Anton Marlovek is my patron."

The merchant shrugged.

"The Marloveks and their ways were fine when it was time to keep the Turks out. These days, though, the Marloveks are a burden on the land." He raised his hand. "The peasants need to be made to work, I'll grant you that, but there are ways and then there are ways. And the ways of the Marloveks are bad."

The coach began to slow. Again, Francois looked out the window.

The threatening purple had nearly blotted out most of the sky, forcing the reddish sunlight to struggle through its murk. The coach slowed to a stop, as Francois noticed a gallows by the side of the road. A bearded man, his arms and legs bound by iron bands, hung from the crossbar, barely swinging.

"Here," the coach driver said. "This is Marlovek land. This is where I leave you."

"Here?" Francois asked.

"Don't be slow." The driver stood up and began pulling Francois' trunk off the roof. "I'm bringing down your trunk."

Francois opened the coach door while the merchant ignored him. He stepped down to the ground and looked at the hanging man.

"Hey! Here!"

The driver shoved the trunk into Francois' hands, making Francois stagger back.

"There's someone coming," the driver said, pointing off into the distance. He turned, picked up his reins, and got the coach moving again, while the merchant pulled the door shut.

Francois let his trunk land on the ground. A carriage indeed was approaching, he could now see, but he wasn't sure it would arrive before the promised storm.

"Are you Christian?"

Francois turned. A tall, bearded man in a black robe, with a long wooden cross on his chest had come out from the woods. The man held the cross by its foot, and Francois noticed that it was an Orthodox cross, with a slanted footrest.

"Are you a Christian?"

"I have been baptized," Francois said. "I am Francois Merillion."

The man's eyebrows arched.

"Frenchman?"

Francois nodded. The man shook his head.

"To learn French is to lose half of one's salvation."

"And who are you?" Francois asked.

"Father Andrei Bogolak," the man said. "The peasants are my flock." He nodded his head toward the oncoming carriage. "The Marloveks are not. They, like you, look to Rome."

Francois thought how to best answer the priest, who then pointed to the body hanging from the gallows.

"The handiwork of the Marloveks, Frenchman."

Again, Francois struggled for words. The priest regarded him with a hostile expression, and Francois stepped away from the man, moving toward the other side of the road.

A whip cracked behind him, and the carriage pulled to a halt between himself and the angry priest. A woman laughed, and the door to the carriage opened.

A young woman in a yellow dress opened the carriage door and smiled at him. She wore her red hair loose upon her shoulders, and her eyes had a mischievous gleam.

"Has Father Andrei been frightening you?" she asked. "You are Francois Merillion, are you not? My brothers will be sad that you have arrived. They have enjoyed their time away from their lessons."

"Are you sad that I have arrived?" Francois asked.

The woman laughed, a musical laugh that both put him at ease yet excited him. She leaned back against her seat, and through the window she no longer blocked, Francois could see the legs of the hanged man.

"I am very glad you have arrived, Monsieur Merillion," she said, and leaned forward again. "I am Katya Marlovek."

She turned her head.

"Borka, rescue Monsieur Merillion's trunk."

She extended her hand to him. "You'll enjoy the ride better inside the carriage. It will storm soon, I believe."

Francois nodded and stepped up to the carriage. As he did, Katya Marlovek leaned back in her seat again, and once more Francois could see the legs of the hanged man.

"Well, are you going to get in?" Katya asked.

Francois took a deep breath as he looked at the hanging man. He glanced away at the lowering skies, then nodded and climbed into the carriage, then pulled the door shut behind him.

"I'm sure it will storm soon," he said.

XXX

"Everyone, the new tutor is here!" Katya called, clapping her hands as she walked into the great room. "Pavel, Timofei, you rascals, come down at once!"

Francois followed her, not wanting to let her get too far ahead of him. His eyes kept darting to the weapons and paintings on the walls.

"Is that banner Turkish?" he asked.

Katya, annoyed, looked over her shoulder.

"Yes, one of grandfather's trophies. From the field of Zenta, I believe." She clapped again. "Pavol! Timofei! Do you want to be birched, you rascals?"

"Katya, child, they are your brothers," a stout woman with a hint of gray in her brown hair said as she entered the room. "Our poor tutor must think we are no better than the Turks or the Russians if you carry on so"

"I would never…" Francois bowed to the woman.

"Anya Marlovek," the woman smiled and extended her hand. Francois kissed it. "I am Katya's aunt."

"A pleasure," Francois said.

"Ah, you Frenchmen lie so skillfully, as if it were no more than breathing," Anya said. "To say it is a pleasure to ride three days east of Sturgik and to see an old woman!" She smiled at Katya. "Keep watch on this one, my dear. He probably knows all kinds of phrases to get what he wants from a girl."

"Madame!" Francois put his hand on his heart. "I…"

"Are you really French?"

Two boys, tightly stuffed into their white breeches and brown jackets, thundered into the room. They halted about a yard from Francois and regarded him with wide eyes. One rushed around to look at Francois' backside.

"He doesn't have a tail!" the boy shouted.

"Timofei, stop showing your ignorance," Anya said. She stamped her foot. "You are deliberately acting up because we have a new tutor. Stop it at once."

"I'm sure the boys and I will reach an understanding," Francois said.

"They need a stiff birching," Katya said, glaring at Timofei.

Francois pointed at a painting on the opposite wall of an armed horseman raising a curved sword against a background of tents.

"With an ancestor like that, one would expect the boys to be spirited."

"The boys, certainly," Anya said. She ran the back of her hand against Katya's sleeve. "That most definitely pleases my brother-in-law."

Katya sighed, stamped her foot and stepped over to the Turkish banner. She favored Francois with a smile and took the banner's edge in her left hand.

"I'm quite sure I'm the reason my father's hair is white."

"If you think you turned my hair white, Katya, you deceive yourself."

Francois turned to the man standing in the doorway. Tall, with deep-set eyes and prominent cheekbones, the man sported a white wig and a black topcoat. His right hand formed a fist as his eyes took in Francois from head to toe and back again.

"You must be hungry to travel so far east from your precious Paris," the man said. "What else could tempt a young popinjay so far from his nest?"

"Are you Count Anton?" Francois asked. He lowered his head to the man. "Thank you for hiring me. I look forward to educating your children."

"I have no doubt you look forward to teaching them more than they look forward to learning from you."

Pavol and Timofei laughed and ran from the room. Anya wrung her hands and sighed.

"Anton, you drive me to despair. This young man has come to us…"

"From France." The Count shook his head. "I know, woman. He has come to eat my bread and take my money, pursing a fruitless errand all the while."

"It is good to have a new face to look at," Katya said, as she favored the tutor with a bright smile.

"Ah." The Count looked as if he wanted to brush Francois away. "What besides trouble comes out of France, I say?" His eyes were cold as he regarded the tutor. "My grandfather carried a French ball in him from the day of Blenheim, and that last war, when we were allies of those wretched popinjays, gained our dear Maria Theresa nothing."

"Hopefully, dear Count, mankind shall outgrow war as children outgrow the toys of their youth." Francois bowed to the older man.

"So you will teach my sons to be idiots?" Count Anton's eyes narrowed. "Mankind devises ever newer toys, but the Old Adam remains a creature of sin and suffering."

"If you believe that, good Count, why did you engage a tutor?" Francois asked.

"Because the Birobachs and the Vistireks have engaged tutors for their children." Count Marlovek made thrusting gestures toward the walls. "And I need to show that I am as grand as they." He scowled at Francois. "You may teach your new ideas to my sons, and no doubt they will learn to parrot them, but they will remain good Marloveks despite all your efforts."

The Count turned from Francois before the young man could respond.

"Let us eat within an hour," he said to Anya. "See to it."

XXX

"Why should we learn French?" Timofei asked.

Francois looked down at the youngster. The boy sat at a desk and seemed genuinely puzzled, unlike his older brother Pavol, who smirked, glad that his brother might be getting into trouble. Timofei scratched his head as he considered his question.

"You will learn the French language to show you are educated," Francois said. "Educated people everywhere speak French."

"Our peasants don't speak French," Pavol said. "You certainly wouldn't want to be mistaken for one of them, do you?"

"Now, now," Francois said.

"Who would mistake me for a peasant?" Timofei asked. He frowned at his brother, who had pressed the back of his hand across his mouth to hide his laughter. "You don't make any sense sometimes, Pavol. I don't think you're as smart as you think you are."

"I'm smarter than you." Pavol sat up straight. "My French is better than yours too."

"I will teach you the words for things that you have in this castle," Francois said. "That way you can remember and use them."

"All right." Timofei smiled.

"Chair – Chaise," Francois said. His eyes went to the wall. "Sword – Epee. Breastplate – Pectoral."

"Curse?" Pavol asked.

"Malediction," Francois said, before realizing what he had said. He frowned and stared at the older boy.

"Wolf?" Pavol asked.

"Loup." Francois frowned at Pavol. "Stop being silly. There is no wolf in the castle. Wolves live in the forest."

"What is the French word for a person who turns into a wolf?" Pavol asked.

"You are being silly," Francois said. Irritation crept into his voice. "There is no such thing as a person who turns into a wolf."

"Nurse said so," Timofei said.

His face was without guile.

"Grandmother stories," Francois said. He shrugged. "There are no such things, even if there are words for them."

"What is the word?" Pavol leaned forward, genuinely curious.

Francois sighed. He looked away and tapped his foot for a moment, then turned back to the eager boy.

"Loup-garou," he said.

The door opened, and Katya stepped into the room. She held a vase of yellow roses.

"Bonjour, Monsieur Merillion," she said.

"Loup-garou," Pavol said. He grinned and tried the word again. "Loup-garou."

"Bonjour," Francois said, as he turned to Katya. "The roses are lovely."

"You seem to have taught my brother a new word," Katya said, as she held the vase out to let Francois sniff the roses. "What does it mean?"

"Loup-garou!" Timofei shouted.

"Just foolishness." Francois shrugged. "The boys asked me the word for werewolf, and I told them."

Katya pulled the vase away from Francois and glared at her brothers.

"Shame on you for wasting your teacher's time! How cruel and foolish you are!"

Francois stepped back from her, amazed at her temper. He smiled at Katya and extended an arm toward her and the other toward her brothers.

"There's no need to get so angry. Boys will be boys."

"They should know better." Her face had gone white. "This is not a matter for joking. Not at all."

Her lips pulled back in pain, and she gasped.

Francois looked at her hand and saw that a thorn had pierced the flesh between her thumb and forefinger. A drop of blood swelled up on her white skin.

"Damn it."

The vase fell from Katya's hand and shattered on the floor, while the yellow roses lost their petals as they struck.

"This is your fault, you monsters," Katya said, thrusting her wounded hand at Timofei.

The boy jumped to his feet, shrieking, and he ran from the room. Pavol, laughing, followed. Katya stared at the mess on the floor.

"They ruined it," she said, then turned and rushed into the hallway.

Francois watched her go, then turned back to the desks where the boys had sat. He took a step toward the door but stopped when he heard the crunch of glass beneath his shoe. Shaking his head, he drew a handkerchief from his pocket, stooped and began to clean up the mess.

XXX

"And what is this place?" Francois asked, as he halted his horse.

He looked at a stout, fire-blackened tower that jutted up at the sky from the top of a steep hill. He noticed gaps in the tower wall and looked down to see several huge stones lying half-buried on the hillside. White clouds passed overhead, making the tower seem darker, more challenging, to their mood.

"This was the first Marlovek castle in these parts," Katya said. "I'm glad I never had to live in it."

She dismounted and led her horse over to a tree, where she tied the reins to a branch. Francois gingerly got down from his mount and followed her to the tree.

"How did it end up like this?" he asked.

Katya shrugged. "Some say the Turks burned it, back in the days of Sulieman the Magnificent. Not that he was here himself. We're too off the beaten track even when catastrophe finds us."

Francois tied his horse's reins to a branch.

"And what do others say?" he asked.

"Foolish things," Katya said, looking away from the castle and rubbing her rose-wounded hand. "Stories that my brothers would believe in."

She gestured at the ruin.

"Some say darkness always follows the Marloveks. Follows and overtakes us. That the Turks did not find it necessary to storm the old castle. They simply burned it so Christians couldn't use it against them. All the Marloveks were dead before they arrived, some say."

Francois looked at the blackened tower. The clouds overhead had become thicker and the sky seemed less welcoming.

"I don't understand."

"My father believes it," Katya said. She turned her back on the ruin. "Vampires. Veshayas. Creatures of darkness." She looked up at Francois. "He believes all of it, and he believes that such creatures have shaped our family."

Blinking, Francois struggled to find something to say.

"Veshaya," Katya said. "It means 'wise one,' but they are wise in the ways of darkness, cunning in the way of evil." She shrugged, and Francois watched her hair bounce on her shoulders. "Or so they claim."

"Such things are only tales told to frighten children, surely," he said.

Katya shook her head.

"Seven years ago, my father heard that an old woman over the hills claimed to be a veshaya. She was predicting the downfall of the Marlovcks. She said the peasants would have the land when we were dead."

"Well," Francois said.

"He captured her and had her burned at the stake." Katya looked beyond Francois, as if her eyes could see the place of execution. "She told him that his daughter would be the downfall of his family. That I would become a wolf and kill them all."

"Oh, dear God." Francois put his arms around Katya and pulled her to his chest.

"You poor girl," he said.

Katya pushed him away.

"My father believes the veshaya spoke the truth," she said. "I see it each time he looks at me. He measures his coffin when he notes how I have grown."

"This is madness," Francois said. He embraced Katya again and kissed the top of her head. "I have to protest this. How can he make your life such agony?"

"He is my father and the Count Marlovek," Katya said. Suddenly, she went limp in the Frenchman's embrace. "I want so much to leave here, to leave this land with its poisoned tales and bitter sayings."

"Oh, Katya," Francois said. "You should be happy."

The wind stirred the branches, and Francois looked up to see that the clouds had turned a somber gray. He sighed and patted Katya's shoulder.

"Let me talk to your father," he said. "There are splendid schools for young ladies in Vienna. Surely he could send you to Sturgik or Randburg even. Anything to get you away from this fog of superstition."

"He will not," Katya said. "He sees me as an enemy, and enemies must be kept under watch." She pulled free from Francois and laughed, a cheerful laugh that ended on a bitter note. "I am his daughter, and not a wolf, but I love him not."

The wind lashed the branches, and the horses started to whinny. Katya rubbed her horse's nose, and Francois, imitating her, did the same to his.

"Let us ride back before the storm comes," he said. "And I will raise the matter with your father. He may see reason yet."

Katya sucked in her cheeks instead of speaking, untied her horse, and quickly mounted the animal. Francois untied his beast, put his foot in the stirrup, took a breath, and then boosted himself to the saddle.

"Let's see if we can outride the storm," Katya said, then she touched her heels to the horse's flanks and galloped away.

XXX

"I understand that you rode to the old castle today," Count Anton Marlovek said, as he cut into the roast pork on the table before him.

"Katya was kind enough to lead me there," Francois said.

Katya and Anya sat facing each other, while the men sat across the table from each other. Three candelabra tried to fend off the darkness.

"Katya finds herself drawn to the old castle," the Count said. His expression became cold. "Even when she is forbidden to go there, she finds her way there."

"It didn't seem especially dangerous to me," Francois said.

"You are a stranger in the land of the Marloveks" The Count put down his knife and fork and pointed at the shadows that flickered on the nearby wall. "You see only mountains and stone and know nothing of the blood that was shed here, or the hatred that still lingers."

"Anton," Anya said.

"You think everything can be explained in those books you have read." The Count's voice got louder, and his sister's shoulders slumped. "But you have not lived among us, Frenchman, or felt the weight of our past on your shoulders."

The Count's fist thumped the table, and the candle flames flickered, making the shadows leap and subside and leap.

"I forbade my daughter from going to the old castle, and she defied me. That is all that matters, Monsieur Merillion."

"Katya is proud of her ancestors, and she showed the old castle to a guest so that he might begin to understand this history of which you speak," Francois said, looking at the Count's plate. He raised his eyes. "She intended nothing wrong."

"I can judge that better than you, Frenchman." The Count scowled. "My wishes were clear, and she defied me."

Katya's face was becoming red as she sat silently and gripped the edge of the table.

"Perhaps your daughter's education would be advanced if you hired a companion for her and sent her to Randburg or Vienna," Francois said. "I don't think the Birobachs or the Vistireks have achieved that distinction yet."

The Count's lips curled in a sour smile, and his teeth could be seen.

"You are a sly one. Are all Frenchmen as sly as you? Surely they must be, or else there would be no stories about sly Frenchmen then." He laughed then regarded the tutor with humorless eyes.

"Not another word on the matter. My daughter is not to go near the old castle, and she most definitely shall not go to Randburg or Vienna, not even in the company of six maiden aunts. Fate cannot be cheated so easily."

Katya's plate hit the floor and shattered. Startled, Francois turned to her as she stood in front of her overturned chair.

"Fate. My fate. You never loved me since that veshaya spoke those words." She ran the back of her hand over her face. "I pity you, father. You have turned me against you."

"It is the power of darkness around us that has done that," Count Anton said.

With a sharp breath, Katya turned and ran from the table. Her feet sounded like thunderbolts as she ran down the hall, to the outer door.

"Mistress Katya," a servant woman called. "Where are you going?"

Katya seized the iron latch with both hands and pulled it back, then shoved the door open.

She ran out into the moonlit night, kicking off her shoes as she ran across the grass. She unbound her hair and let it fly freely behind her, as the moon's yellow light spilled across her angry face.

She breathed deeply of the night air, yet she could not pull in enough. Something pounded in her head, gripped at her throat. She slipped on the grass and tumbled forward, hitting the ground and rolling over until she landed on her back.

Katya looked up at the sky. Never had the moon looked so large to her or seemed so dire. She rolled again and buried her face in the grass. Her hands grabbed two tufts and yanked them free as she wept.

"Katya!"

It was that fool of a Frenchman.

"Katya!"

She sprang to her feet and ran again, not wanting him to see her like this, not wanting to see him this night.

Her heart pounded in her chest like it never had before. Strange new smells assaulted her, and she wept. She ran faster as her clothes gripped and clung to her body.

She snarled at the discomfort and tore at her sleeves.

"Katya!" Once more the Frenchman called to her.

She howled in reply.

XXX

Weak, orange light began to peek around the eastern hills, as Francois threw his arm around a birch and leaned against its trunk. He breathed through his mouth and felt the air burn his chest. His feet ached. He closed his eyes.

He heard a moan.

Eyes suddenly open, Francois stood still for an instant, not quite believing he had heard anything but the rushing of a stream. He blinked, then blinked again. His face relaxed, and then he heard the moan again.

He pushed himself away from the tree and began walking unsteadily down the hill toward the stream.

"Are you there, Katya?" he asked the twilight.

His knees shook and he nearly fell to the ground, but a third time the moan came to him. He pulled his energy together and ran down toward the rushing water.

Even in the dismal light, he could see her pale flesh and the rags of the yellow dress she had worn the night before. She lay face down at the edge of the stream, one arm and one leg in the rushing water.

Francois pulled off his jacket as he hurried down the slope and threw it on the bank. Then he stood over her, reached under her arms, and pulled her away from the stream. She moaned again as he moved her, and he lay her down, then lay his jacket over her back.

He pressed a hand to her cheek. It felt quite hot.

"Katya," he said, nearly bursting into tears.

Her face had been placid until the mention of her name. At that moment, she shook with agitation, lifted her head, and shrieked.

Francois put his left hand on her shoulder.

"It's I, Francois," he said. "You are safe. Thank the good Lord, you are safe. When you are ready, I'll take you back to the castle."

Katya shook like a reed in a fire. She lifted her head and looked at Francois.

"Better I should have drowned."

He put the back of his hand against her cheek.

"Don't say such things. It has been a horrible night for all of us."

More orange light stretched into the valley where they were. The shadows pulled back into the rocks and holes.

"I…" Katya closed her eyes. "I…" She opened her eyes and looked at Francois, then shook her head. "But how could I?

She pulled her right hand around before her face and looked at it, turning it over and back again. She blinked.

"It was a dream," Katya said at last. "It must have been a dream."

"What?"

Katya shook her head.

"No," she said. "Madness."

She pulled Francois' jacket around her chest and sat up. She looked away from him.

"I cannot stay here," she said. "Or I will go mad. That was what last night proved. My father's sickness. His stories, his beliefs. They have created a sickness in my soul. And if I don't get away, it will destroy me."

Francois rubbed her cheek.

"Katya, I will get you away from here, away from him."

She grabbed his hand with her left hand and gazed into his eyes.

"It must be tonight, Francois," she said. "Another night like this, and there will be nothing of me left. I will be mad or damned."

"But we need to arrange for a chaperone for you," Francois said. "If we ran from here tonight, your father would hunt us down. He'd have me hanged and he'd make you a prisoner within your own walls. And if he did not catch us, we could never live like respectable folk."

Katya lowered her head and released his hand.

"You are right, of course, Francois." She sighed. "A chaperone must be at hand or else we would live little better than beasts."

Katya laughed. Francois put his hand on her shoulder.

"It will work out," he said. "It will."

Katya stood up and clutched the jacket around her. She sighed and then began walking into the sunlight, toward the castle.

Francois stood up and hurried after her.

XXX

Francois' pen stopped as the peasant walked over the narrow bridge.

This was the third peasant who had crossed the lonely footbridge in the last ten minutes, Francois thought as he leaned his head back against the birch tree.

He had come to this spot to sketch the bridge because it had been a solitary place, and he needed to get away from the tension in the castle. Katya came to meals but only picked at her food, something that spurred her father's anger. Anya burst into tears at the first hint of tension, and Pavol and Timofei refused their lessons and enjoyed their tutor's frustration.

Francois had sketched the Marloveks' mill, several Marlovek horses, and the old castle itself. Finding this narrow bridge that arched above a rapid spot in the stream had raised his spirits, as he imagined the hours he could spend sketching it, time away from the mare's nest of emotions in the castle.

Today, however, many peasants seemed to be using this bridge, he noted. They were always men, and rather young men at that.

Francois scratched the cleft of his chin with the end of his pen as he thought about the peasants. He finally closed his sketchbook, put it in his jacket pocket, and then walked toward the path as quietly as he could.

These peasants didn't seem as if they were up to no good, but something about them made him uneasy.

Francois walked to the side of the path as it ascended a ridge and dipped down into a copse of trees. He stopped and took a breath.

Had the peasants been doing anything wrong? he asked himself. They had as much right to walk this path as he had. What had he hoped to find anyway?

"The Marloveks will destroy us."

Francois turned his heard toward the sound he had heard. He pressed himself against the trunk of an oak and listened.

"They have had their foot on our necks for years," a man said. "But this latest. It can't be tolerated."

"A wolf killed old Grigor," a younger man said. "How can you blame the Marloveks for what a wolf does?"

"Have you forgotten Wise Anna?" the first man asked. "Have you? The Marloveks hanged her, but she warned us that a wolf would come from the House of Marlovek and destroy us. That was seven years ago. You may have forgotten, but I, Olgerd, have not."

Francois could hear some muttering.

"Grigor was my friend," Olgerd said. "And he lies dead because of a Marlovek."

"What are we to do?" another man asked.

Olgerd made a sound of disgust.

"In my grandfather's day, men were not so cowardly. They rose up under Khlastkov and fought the aristocrats."

"And Khlastkov died on the iron hook, and the aristocrats have had their foot upon our necks heavier still." There was much murmuring at this. "You talk a good fight, Olgerd, but others will pay in blood."

Francois stepped away from the tree and began taking long, silent strides away from the peasants toward the castle.

All the more reason to take Katya away from here, he thought.

XXX

"You are quiet tonight, Frenchman," Count Anton said. He dabbed at his mouth with a linen napkin. "Usually you do not lack for words."

"I am sorry if my silence displeases you," Francois said. He put his fork down. "I know that my conversation sometimes angers you."

The Count raised a hand. "I have been on battlefields against the Prussians and the Turks. If I let the words of a Frenchman bother me, I would never have lived to see my hair turn white." He took a sip of wine. "Do you know why Katya did not join us for dinner tonight?"

Francois glanced at the empty chair.

"I have no idea, good Count. Perhaps she does not feel well."

The hint of a smile played around the Count's lips, but there was no mirth in his eyes.

"Perhaps. Or perhaps she intends me to think that she is unwell."

Francois took a sip of his wine. "And why should she do that?"

"I can think of several reasons," the Count said. His hand closed around the stem of his goblet. He began to turn it in his grasp. "You think Katya should go from here, don't you?"

Francois swallowed. He glanced at Anya, who avoided looking at him.

"I believe Katya should get away from this place and its talk of a curse on the family," he said. "She can have no joy here."

"Joy?" The Count laughed, a cold, bark-like laugh. "What joy can be found in this land of hatred and dark spirits? My ancestors kept the Turks out of this place, and we are hated for it. If we Marloveks did not make them work, the peasants would go back to living in the woods like bears. Less than bears because they cannot catch their own food.

"You, Frenchman, are a fool. You think ideas dreamed up in Paris will flourish in the soil of Bavaria, Austria, Hungary, and Kurgania." He shook his head. "You might see some weak shoots break forth, but the soil here is rich in the blood of the damned. Any idea that does not recognize the hatred and the whip and the curse upon this land is doomed to grow misshapen and die unmourned."

The Count pointed at Francois.

"You shall never take Katya from here. I will see to that. She is a Marlovek, and she will die in these hills without seeing your precious Enlightenment."

"How can you believe this?" Francois asked.

"I am the Count Marlovek!"

The Count swung his arm to strike his chest, and the wine goblet fell over. Its red contents splashed out upon the white linen tablecloth, thrusting one weak arm toward the Frenchman, while the bulk of the wine formed a stain that rushed at the Count.

Count Anton stared at the pattern that aimed at his heart, and his face grew pale.

"So be it," he said, his voice barely louder than a whisper.

"So be it," he said, more loudly, standing up and pushing his chair back with his legs. With a clatter, the chair fell backward, and the Count turned away from the table and strode off, out of the dining room, his motion setting all the candles to guttering.

"What?" Francois asked.

"Go now," Anya said, as she looked at the stain. "He is very disturbed and will be thinking about this for a while."

"But what?"

Anya looked at the Frenchman.

"If you are going to rescue Katya, tonight is the night. Do it now, for Anton will never be so distracted. If you believe she can be saved, take her far from this place and its talk of curses. If you fail to try, may you burn in hell with the worst sinners."

Francois felt his mouth go dry. He stood up and pushed his chair back.

"Of course," he said. "Thank you."

"Be off with Katya tonight," Anya said. Her gaze turned back to the wine stain on the white tablecloth. "Waste no time."

XXX

The wind rose, beating the grass and moving the thin, pale clouds across the face of the wide, white moon. Francois gripped Katya's hand and kept her from falling.

"The bridge is not far," he said. "Just down this slope." He caught his breath. "We're almost off Marlovek land by that point."

Katya was not listening to him. Her eyes turned to the moon, then back to the castle. She pressed her hand against her heart and shook her head.

"Francois, I will not be able to leave this land of the Marloveks. It is too late for me. If you had come a year earlier, perhaps, but now it is too late for me."

Francois put his hands on her shoulders. Her face was pale and empty of hope and she did not even raise her eyes to his. Francois tried to smile.

"It is just the stories you've heard and this dismal night in these legend-shrouded hills. Tomorrow morning, Katya, when we have crossed the river and left these forests, life will look different. You'll see then there is no Marlovek curse, only a sickness in your mind."

He kissed her unresponsive lips.

"A sickness that will leave you without a trace," Francois said, "once we get you away from here."

"Oh, Francois," she said. "Can't you see that it is too late?"

She pointed back toward the castle. Francois fought down the impulse to argue with her, and looked where she pointed.

A tall, white-haired man, his scarlet-lined cloak blowing behind him and his silver-headed walking stick catching the moonlight, strode toward the lovers. His pace did not vary.

Francois turned and pulled at Katya's arm. She did not budge. He turned and scooped her up and began running to the bridge as fast as he could.

Katya did not embrace him but remained aloof in his arms. His foot struck a tree root, and he nearly stumbled. He kept hold of Katya and started to run to the wooden structure.

"It is the Marlovek blood, Katya, that enslaves you to this bitter land!"

The Count's words sounded like thunder.

"She has killed, Frenchman. Did you know that? Did you know that she has run on all fours and slain? Even if you take her to Paris, her guilty blood will flow through her veins and she will be a werewolf."

Only now did Katya grab Francois' jacket.

"It's true," she said. "I have killed."

"No," he said. "You could not."

But even as he spoke the words, he could see that her face was darker. Her hair had grown longer, and her eyebrows had met. Her lips pulled back to reveal sharp teeth.

"Too late, Francois," she said. "Too late."

"Katya!"

She sprang from the Frenchman's arms, as the old aristocrat charged down the slope at them. Moonlight made the orb at the end of his walking stick, which he raised like a weapon, glow in the night sky.

"No!" Francois rushed between father and daughter.

The silver orb crashed down, striking the side of his head. Francois grabbed at the Count's jacket, but the Count thrust the orb into the younger man's chest. Francois gasped as all the air went out of his lungs, and he fell.

Over and over he rolled, as the rushing sound of the stream came closer.

Behind him, Francois could hear the shriek of a wolf and the defiant roar of a man who knew he would die.

XXX

"Leave us, Frenchman," Father Andrei said.

He stood at the foot of the burned gallows. He pointed at the road.

"Be away from here and forget the cursed Marloveks. Their destiny is not yours. Your destiny is not theirs. Be away from here and think of them no more."

His head and right arm bandaged, Francois did not meet the priest's gaze. He only looked past the empty, blackened gallows as if trying to see the castle of the Marloveks. Finally, he shook his head, turned away from the priest, and began walking along the empty road.

Cursed

Frank gripped the handlebars and peddled. He could smell the new rubber of the grips. His hands would smell funny the rest of the day, but he didn't care.

He peddled to the end of the driveway and stopped. Four houses down, several children stood around a tall kid with a blue bicycle. A girl and a boy who seemed about his age looked at him.

Smiling, Frank waved at them and turned his bike right. He rode down the sidewalk to the kids, bringing his bike to a neat stop.

"Hi," he said.

"Hi," the girl said. A boy with the same black hair nudged her.

"I'm Frank." He looked at them. Four boys and two girls. The boy on the bike was the oldest, maybe twelve. The others were about his age or younger, like the girl who had talked. They didn't say anything to him now. The older boy looked at Frank's bike and didn't smile.

"You're new," another boy said. "You live in the Staudter house?"

"Yes. That's my grandfather's."

"How come you don't go to school?" a different boy asked.

"I go to school," Frank said. "I go to the Lutheran school."

"Thought so," said the older boy. He chewed his thumb. "So what does your father do for a living?"

"I don't know," Frank said. "My father doesn't live with us."

The other kids looked at each other. "I told you so," said the boy on his bike.

He put down the kickstand and got off. He walked over to Frank and smiled.

"We're not going to play with you." He looked around at the other kids, who nodded or looked away. He turned back to Frank. "So you can just ride on by, but we're not going to play with you."

He turned and walked back to his bicycle and got on. He looked at Frank. The other kids, even the girl who had talked to Frank earlier, now looked away. Frank bit his lips and started peddling. He went down to the end of the block, stopped, crossed the street, and went back up the other side until he was across from his driveway. The other kids watched him all the way.

Frank looked both ways, crossed the street and rode his bike up to the garage. He got off, walked it inside, and then went in the house.

XXX

Frank saw Pastor Graeber shaking hands with Mrs. Schulz, who had a long story to tell him, so he quickly stepped out of the line, walked behind those waiting for the Pastor and hurried into the parking lot. He smiled when he saw Ed walking to his parents' car.

"Hey, Ed!"

Ed turned around and waited as Frank ran up.

"How was The Black Tower?"

"It was good. Grenzel was terrific." Ed blinked. "Why didn't you watch it?"

Frank looked back over his shoulder for a moment. "My mom says horror movies are bad for kids. So I had to watch Lawrence Welk with her. What's going to be on Creature Feature next week?"

Ed made a face. "Curse of the Man Wolf. Joe saw it last

year, and he says it's a big cheat. There's no werewolf in it at all. It's about some kid --"

"Frank!" Frank's Mom stood at the entrance to the church and looked around. "Frank Kurganak!"

"I better get back to her," Frank said. "Have a good week."

"You too," Ed said, walking off to his parents' car.

Frank turned and walked back to his mom. The thing about summer was that he could only see his friends on Sundays.

XXX

Frank stared at the TV. Dennis the Menace and Tommy had ridden their bikes over to Margaret's lemonade stand. Margaret tossed her curly hair back and said that Mr. Wilson was mad at Dennis.

"You watching TV again?" his grandfather asked as from the living room doorway.

Frank looked up at him. "Yes."

"It's a sunny day. Go out and ride your bike. Play with some other kids for once."

Frank stood up and walked over to the TV. "Okay." He shut off the TV and walked through the kitchen and out the door.

It was a sunny day. He walked his bicycle out of the garage and ran his hand over the seat a couple of times to get rid of the dust. Then he hopped on and rode to the end of the driveway. He stopped and looked around.

Someone had put up a lemonade stand down the street on the other side. Frank remembered the TV show, laughed at the coincidence and peddled across the street, then rode over to the stand.

Two dark-haired girls sat on black card table chairs behind a huge pitcher of lemonade. A stack of several Styrofoam cups stood off to the side, and several dried sticky spots dotted the top of the card table.

"How much?" Frank asked.

The two girls looked at him, and then they looked at each other. They turned back to him, and then the older girl asked:

"Are your parents divorced?"

Frank swallowed.

"Yes."

"Oh," she said, blinking rapidly.

They looked at him some more and didn't say anything. Frank felt his face getting hot, and he gripped his handlebars until the palms of his hand hurt.

"Forget it," he said and rode away.

XXX

Frank took <u>Daniel Boone Frontiersman</u> off the shelf and slipped the list out from where he'd hidden it at the back of the book. Just looking at the piece of paper made him smile and feel good.

He'd asked Ed for a list of the best horror movies, and Ed had written down a bunch of titles, running from top to bottom on a three-ring notebook page. Frank had only seen a handful, each duly marked by a check.

Ed hadn't been sure of the order to put the movies in, which ones came before others. Frank had really enjoyed listening to Ed and his brother Joe arguing about whether <u>Ghost of Frankenstein</u> came before <u>Frankenstein Meets the Man Wolf</u> or not. It would just be so cool to have someone living in the same house who liked the same stuff you did, he thought.

There were a lot of <u>Son of</u>, <u>Bride of</u> and <u>House of</u> titles on the list, he thought as he looked at it again.

He had an idea. He ran to the living room and took a pencil out of the desk drawer, then hurried back to his room. He grabbed <u>Daniel Boone Frontiersman</u> and jumped up on the bed, placing the book across his lap. Carefully, and with reverence, he put the list atop the book.

<u>Bride of Frankenstein</u>, he read a couple of lines down. He moved his pencil to the other side of the page and on the same line wrote <u>Bride of Kurganak</u> and underlined it.

He looked at the title and smiled. It worked. It sounded real, as if there was a book or movie with that title somewhere. His smile widened.

<u>Kurganak's Daughter</u> soon flowed from his pencil. Then <u>Son of Kurganak</u>, <u>Ghost of Kurganak</u>, <u>House of Kurganak</u>, and <u>Curse of Kurganak</u>.

The last one made him frown. Curse and Kurganak both started with the same sound, and that made the title almost sound silly. He erased Kurganak and wrote <u>Curse of Staudter</u>. That sounded better.

Frank lay back on his bed. He could see it now. Castle Kurganak looming on the mountaintop. Baron Kurganak would be a vampire, who would descend to the village each night to drink the blood of the villagers. Or maybe the ancestral curse was being a werewolf. When the full moon rose, the oldest male Kurganak would sprout fur and hunt for victims.

Frank frowned. That was kind of far-fetched, he thought, but maybe one of the Kurganaks had dug up bodies and stitched the parts together to create a Monster. That was the kind of thing that might have actually happened. And the peasants rebelled and burned the castle, and that's why the Kurganaks had to move to America.

That's why the kids don't like you, he thought. They know.

They watch the same movies, and they know.

XXX

"So Frankie," Grandpa Staudter said, "I saw in the paper that your friend died."

Frank dropped his fork. "Who died?"

"Don't play with the boy like that," Mom said to him. She turned to Frank. "Karl Grenzel died. That's all."

"Frankie likes his movies," Grandpa said.

"I didn't even know Karl Grenzel was still alive." Mom looked at Frank's plate. "Eat your beans."

"Of course he was still alive. He did the voice for that Christmas special last year." Grandpa took a sip of coffee.

"Well, I'd hate to have a life based on scaring people," Mom said. "That's no kind of life at all for a decent person to have."

"Can I see the article?" Frank asked.

"What?" Grandpa looked puzzled. "Oh, I guess so. It didn't say much more than that he died. Except that he changed his name to go into movies."

"From what?" Frank asked.

"What do you care, from what?" Grandpa laughed. "It's not like he was a relative, and we're going to inherit anything."

Frank took a forkful of beans and ate for a while. Grandpa sipped his coffee. Frank looked out the window, then turned back to the old man.

"So why did our ancestors come to America?" he asked. "Did they have to leave?"

"America is the land of freedom," Mom said.

"No, I mean did people burn down their castle?"

"What?" Grandpa asked.

"Did the peasants get angry because there was a monster or werewolf attacks or something like that?" Frank looked at his grandfather and hoped for the truth. "Is that why they had to leave the Old Country?"

Grandpa laughed and shook his head. "There never was a castle."

"What a horrible thing to think!" Mom glared at Frank. "You come from respectable people. Do you hear me? Respectable." She turned to her father. "This is what comes from letting him watch those dreadful movies and talking about Karl Grenzel at the dinner table. If he talks like this in front of anyone else, they'll think I'm a bad mother for letting him watch such things."

Grandpa laughed. "A castle. Schloss Staudter. If only there had been such a thing." He wiped his eyes.

Mom held her finger in front of Frank's face.

"You will never watch those dreadful movies again."

XXX

Frank held the soapy kettle under the trickle of water until all the suds were gone. He looked at the clock. 7:25.

"Thank you for helping with the dishes, Frankie," Aunt Lottie said. "You're a very good boy."

Frank smiled. "I try, Aunt Lottie."

His grandfather's sister stretched her back and groaned before she put a hand on his shoulder and propelled him from the kitchen sink to the dining room.

"What shall we do before your mother picks you up?" She walked over to the drawer where she kept the playing cards. "Would you like to play some Michigan?"

Frank looked at the clock again.

"Aunt Lottie, could I watch <u>Creature Feature</u>?"

The old woman looked puzzled for a moment, then her face brightened.

"Oh, Fritz had said there was something that happened. So that's why you wanted to come over here tonight."

Frank couldn't look at her.

"I do like coming over, Aunt Lottie. I did dust the floors and carry out the old newspapers."

"And now you want to watch some TV show."

Frank nodded. "Yes."

Aunt Lottie laughed. "Well, good work should be rewarded. You can watch, but I will watch too, and if I don't like it, off it goes."

"Great."

Frank ran into the living room and turned the knob on Aunt Lottie's new TV.

"What channel is it on?" she asked as she walked into the room.

"Channel 61."

"The channels don't go up that high," she said.

"It's UHF," Frank said, turning the top dial to the UHF slot and then turning the bottom dial.

"What are you doing?" Aunt Lottie asked. "I never touch

that dial."

"It's started already," Frank said as the picture became clear.

XXX

A boy in a conical paper hat sat alone at an outdoor table beneath criss-crossed streams of crepe paper. A dozen plates of melting ice cream stretched around the table from him. Angry adult voices came up from behind.

"Why isn't anyone here?" a man asked. "Did you send those invitations?"

"I sent the invitations," a woman said. "They just didn't come."

"What a waste," the man said. "Why is he so unpopular? I had friends when I was a kid. I had plenty of friends."

XXX

"What are you watching?" Mom asked as she stepped into the living room. "You're watching <u>Creature Feature,</u> aren't you? That's why you wanted to come to Aunt Lottie's and help out this afternoon."

"It's all right, Annie," Aunt Lottie said, getting out of her chair. "This show isn't anything to get worked up over."

"I should have known better," Mom said, walking over to the TV. "Sneaking around behind my back."

"Annie, leave the TV on," Aunt Lottie said.

Frank looked at his aunt. Never had he heard her so angry.

"Come out to the kitchen and talk to me about this." Aunt Lottie took his Mom by the hand. "Come. I'll warm up the coffee."

The two women left the room, and Frank continued to watch.

XXX

The birthday boy stood, without his hat, in the yard of a big, dark house. The walls were black, and each window seemed to have its own roof.

"Who's been nibbling at my house?" an old woman asked as she stepped out of the shadows.

The boy looked as if he wanted to run away, but then the old woman laughed and waved at him.

"Forgive an old actress her tricks." She moved fully into the light and looked small and frail. "I'm not a witch, and no matter what it looks like, this house isn't gingerbread."

XXX

"Nobody takes me seriously!"

Frank turned from the TV to look at the kitchen. His Mom had never raised her voice like that before.

"Now, Annie, we all love you, and we know this is very painful," Aunt Lottie said. "Always remember that we love you."

"I don't want him watching those movies! I'm his mother!"

Frank turned back to the TV.

XXX

The old woman and the boy now stood indoors, in a dark room with one window and one lamp. A wolf-skin rug lay on the floor, and two wolf-head trophies thrust out from the wall.

"Perhaps your father was a werewolf," the old woman said.

"It is a very old curse. Ancient. Some say it goes back to Nebuchadnezzar or even to Cain. Those who bear the curse are shunned by the rest of mankind. The hand of all is raised against them. None dare give a werewolf comfort."

XXX

"We're going now," Mom said as she marched into the living room and grabbed Frank by the hand. "Say goodnight to Aunt Lottie."

"Goodnight, Aunt Lottie," Frank said as he stood up. "Goodbye."

"Goodnight, Frankie," Aunt Lottie said. "We'll see each other again. I'll have you back over."

"Just not on a Saturday," Mom said, and she led Frank to the door.

XXX

Moonlight poured through Frank's window and made the sheets glow at the bottom of his bed. Frank tossed back and forth. How did the movie end? What happened to the boy? Maybe Ed would tell him tomorrow, but it didn't sound like Ed would have watched the movie. Maybe Ed wouldn't be at church at all.

Frank looked at the moonlight at the bottom of his bed. He wriggled his toes and made the glowing sheets move. Before he fell asleep, Frank thought of how much the moonlight made the crumpled sheets look like snow.

And then he stood in the snow, halfway up a mountain. From below him, came the happy sounds of Lawrence Welk and canned laughter. Frank looked down the road to the village, where snow covered the lemonade stands and draped the TV antennas on top of the peasants' homes. They were wrapped in mirth, he knew, but they would not have any mirth or fellowship to spare for him.

Frank looked up the mountain to the looming turrets of Castle Kurganak. Lightning struck the metallic spires that rose into the night sky, sending spirals of white sparks cascading downward. Meanwhile a piercing howl echoed from the bowls of the dungeon and made the hair on Frank's neck stand up.

With a rusty shriek, the castle's massive wooden door swung open, and a row of torches flared invitingly in the darkness.

Without a look back at the village, Frank hurried up the rest of the mountain way to Castle Kurganak. He did not pause when he reached the huge door but strode into the darkness without hesitation, to dwell with the monsters.

Never Be Rid of Him: Thoughts on Val Lewton

Since the 1960s, talk about classic Hollywood cinema has to
deal with the "auteur theory," the idea that directors were able to
stamp their own personality on movies from the "dream factory."
Directors such as John Ford, Howard Hawks, Alfred Hitchcock, and
John Huston became the subject of serious study.

It is much rarer for a producer to become an artistic hero.
The stereotype of a Hollywood producer is a cigar-chomping tyrant
who only cares about money and sexual favors. However, against
the odds, three men have emerged as "auteur" producers: Arthur
Freed, Mark Hellinger, and Val Lewton. Of the three, Freed is the
most famous, the man responsible for most of the great MGM
musicals of the Forties and Fifties, films such as <u>Meet Me in St.
Louis</u>, <u>Singin' in the Rain</u>, and <u>The Bandwagon</u>. Mark Hellinger is
the most obscure, perhaps because he moved from Warner Brothers
to Universal, but devotees of the crime film admire him for <u>The
Roaring Twenties</u>, <u>High Sierra</u>, <u>The Killers</u>, and <u>The Naked City</u>.
Enjoying a level of fame between Freed and Hellinger is Val
Lewton, cherished for the horror movies he made for RKO from
1942 to 1946.

Perhaps it is not surprising that Freed, Hellinger, and Lewton
stand out as creative among producers, since each was a creator
before becoming a producer. Freed was a songwriter, and "Singin' in
the Rain" was one of his compositions. Hellinger had been a famous
newspaper columnist in New York City. By contrast, Lewton was
the least successful of the three before turning to film. He had
published several short stories and novels that achieved only a
middling success at best. <u>No Bed of Her Own</u>, a "steamy" novel by
the standards of 1931, was his biggest success and was filmed the

next year as <u>No Man of Her Own</u>, but Lewton's next three novels failed to strike a spark, and so the struggling novelist went into the movies.

Val Lewton's fame rests on the horror movies he produced, and much of his legend depends on the contrast between the cultured man Lewton, the son of a Russian ballerina, was and the lurid-sounding titles of the films he produced. Indeed, Lewton's wife was quoted in <u>Look</u> magazine as saying that she would only see one of her husband's movies if forced to the theater by a tank.

The legend of Lewton also makes great play out of how Lewton subverted the titles he was given. The prime example is <u>Curse of the Cat People</u> (1944), directed by Robert Wise, which ended up lyrical and not lurid, a sensitive psychological study of a lonely child. Indeed, a generation of two of film critics delighted in praising Lewton, using his films as a stick to beat the rest of the genre, particularly Universal's movies. In this tradition, it was claimed that Lewton's films were "psychological" (and thus good) instead dealing with the "supernatural" (and thus bad). It was asserted that <u>Cat People</u> (1942), directed by Jacques Tourneur was about a woman who thought she would turn into a panther, but really couldn't, as opposed to <u>The Wolf Man</u>, which was about the preposterous idea that a man could turn into a wolf. Because <u>The Wolf Man</u> showed us a man turning into a wolf, it was obviously inferior to <u>Cat People</u>, which had no transformation scene.

To be blunt, this is a misreading of <u>Cat People</u>. There was no transformation scene because Lewton realized his unit could not duplicate the effect that Universal had achieved in <u>The Wolf Man</u>. Instead, the transformation of Irena to a panther is suggested. Footprints show that Irena (Simone Simon) has become a panther, and when her body is found in the zoo, her husband (Kent Smith) speaks the last line of the movie: "She never lied to us." This means that Irena was right; she could turn into a panther.

This essay is an attempt to save Lewton from some of his admirers. It will point out where Lewton doesn't hold up as well as draw attention to overlooked places where he excelled. Indeed, Lewton pioneered some aspects of the horror film that some of his admirers would like to shun. Lewton's films for RKO are (mostly) a treasure for the horror fan, but a person can like them and like Universal's output as well.

Perhaps the place where I part company with most Lewton enthusiasts is his second film, I Walked with a Zombie (1943), directed by Jacques Tourneur. To many, this is Lewton's best film. In my eyes, it is something of a mess.

Typically, when I see a movie, my attitude toward it doesn't change much even on subsequent viewings. I Walked with a Zombie is a major exception. I first saw this film when I was about 13, and I found it insufferably boring. Eight years later, I was deeply impressed with its moodiness. Twenty years after that, I found it stuffy and ashamed of being a horror movie.

The movie tries to do too much in too little time and strikes me as afraid of its own themes. Yes, Sir Lancelot's calypso singer is an unforgettable character and miles removed from how African-Americans were usually depicted in Hollywood horror movies of the Thirties and Forties. Yet the movie's "scary face" is a black zombie, and the voodoo ceremony that is the destination of the admittedly scary and poetic walk of the title turns out to be stage managed by the (white) mother of the plantation owner so she can get the islanders to take modern medicine. That undercuts a lot of the dignity of the islanders that Sir Lancelot's performance created.

Also, the plot is supposedly driven by passion, which I can't detect. The protagonist, a nurse (Frances Dee) who comes to island to care for the wife of a plantation owner, finds herself drawn to the owner (Tom Conway), who is her employer. She discovers that her patient actually had an affair with the owner's half-brother before she sank into a coma. This affair is safely in the past and is only referred to by dialogue from secondary characters, while the nurse and her employer keep everything quite proper between them until the adulterous couple perishes. Thus, I Walked with a Zombie never really generates any heat despite its story being (supposedly) driven by two "forbidden loves."

The titular walk to the voodoo ceremony is certainly spooky, only to have its atmosphere undercut by the presence of the plantation owner's mother. The climactic doom of the adulterous lovers is very poetic, but it would have more punch if we had ever seen them as lovers, instead of having the "evil woman" be in a coma for the whole film. Apart from these two sequences, I Walked With a Zombie doesn't generate much emotion for me.

Indeed, I suspect that Val Lewton and Jacques Tourneur realized that they had been too genteel in I Walked With a Zombie, because their next movie, The Leopard Man (1943), would be a surprisingly violent horror film for the era, with the deaths of three female characters being pretty merciless.

The first death is so powerful, in fact, that it comes as a surprise to realize that the scene still isn't that well known. A Hispanic girl is sent out after dark by her harsh mother to buy flour even though an escaped leopard is loose in the town. The girl manages to buy flour, sees the leopard, and runs home. As she bangs on the door and screams to be let in, her mother mocks her fears, until the leopard can be heard. When the mother tries to open the door, the lock is jammed, and the girl's blood runs under the door. Having the victim die on the other side of the door is, perhaps, "suggest don't show," but Lewton and Tourneur show more blood in this scene than Universal did in all its monster films put together.

The second death could fit into a slasher movie of the Eighties. A teenage girl goes to the cemetery for a secret meeting with her boyfriend. She arrives late, finds that he has gone, and sits down and feels sorry for herself. The caretaker locks her in the cemetery. When the girl realizes her plight, she wanders around the cemetery beneath a full moon until she is murdered. In a way, this almost anticipates the slasher movie "code" of bad girls who want to be sexually active get murdered.

With the exception of Curse of the Cat People, subsequent Lewton films also display a good amount of violence and cruelty. In The Seventh Victim, the emphasis is on psychological pressure placed on a woman who wishes to leave a Satanic cult. The cultists try to drive her to suicide, and, shockingly, at the end of the film they succeed. How Lewton got away with the ending is puzzling to me, but I appreciate whatever horse-trading he endured to win this extremely chilly climax.

Unusual and violent deaths can be found in many of Lewton's films. In The Ghost Ship (1943), directed by Mark Robson, a sailor is locked in a room and crushed by an anchor chain, while in Bedlam (1946), directed by Mark Robson, an asylum inmate suffocates when he is painted gold for a masquerade. The Ghost Ship also includes a knife fight that shows blood, but easily the most violent of Lewton's films is The Body Snatcher (1945), directed by Robert Wise. Lewton had both Bela Lugosi and Boris Karloff in this film, and both horror stars got suitably grim send-offs, in particular Karloff's character who dies after a long, grueling fight scene remarkable for its intensity.

So, despite the claims of some of his champions, Lewton included a lot of violence in his films and was not averse to showing blood. However, his films never seem mere examples of exploitation, because they are filled with interesting characters that catch your attention because of the care invested in them, whether the cleaning woman in <u>Cat People</u> or the lunatic in <u>Bedlam</u> who might be the unacknowledged great-grandfather of the motion picture industry.

Not everything in Lewton films work. <u>The Seventh Victim</u> (1943), directed by Mark Robson, is crippled by the weakness of two of its three male performances. Dr. Judd, the third male character in <u>The Seventh Victim</u>, is well played by Tom Conway, but Dr. Judd had been killed at the end of <u>Cat People</u>. So, either <u>The Seventh Victim</u> takes place earlier, and Dr. Judd became corrupt by the time of <u>Cat People</u>, or Judd's presence in the <u>The Seventh Victim</u> is a joke on us. Either way, his presence in the 1943 film is a distraction. Likewise, <u>Isle of the Dead</u> (1945), directed by Mark Robson, despite having one of the most terrifying "Lewton walks" ever, suffers from an unfocused plot. Despite these shortcomings, Lewton's horror films, with their serious outlook and steadfast refusal to play the horror elements for laughs, always remind us that horror movies can strike us at a deep level and always remain with us.

Here are several things I love about the films of Val Lewton.

First, I love <u>Cat People</u>. If you read a one-sentence plot description of this film, you might think this was the most "square" and chauvinistic film Hollywood ever made. Oliver marries Irena, a foreign woman, who carries an evil curse that is brought out by Dr. Judd, her wicked psychologist. The movie ends with the evil foreign woman and deceitful intellectual dead, and Oliver is free to wed the normal American girl.

And yet, despite such a conformist plot, the movie lavishes sympathy on Irena. She manages to be both the monster of the movie and its most sympathetic character. <u>Cat People</u> makes us well aware of what Irena's exclusion from the happy American life everyone around her is demanding of Irena. Any viewer who has ever felt excluded from anything sympathizes with Irena and her plight. This clash between its square plot and sympathetic execution gives Cat People its evocative qualities and keeps viewers coming back to the film, like Irena keeps returning to the panther cage.

Another thing I love about Lewton's legacy is "the Lewton walk." In most Lewton movies, there is a sequence in which a character takes a walk through the menacing dark. The practice began in Cat People, when Alice, the normal American woman, walks to a bus stop and begins to become aware that something is following her in the darkness. Even when one knows that Alice will survive this ordeal, this first "Lewton walk" builds tension. (The tension is released when a bus squeals to a halt and opens its door, a sound that initially the viewer takes for a panther's snarl. The "bus," the fake scare, has since become a cliché. The "Lewton walk," which takes a lot of planning, is usually forgotten.)

Memorable "Lewton walks" followed in I Walked with a Zombie, The Leopard Man, and The Seventh Victim. Even though Isle of the Dead had an interrupted production and is, to me, perhaps Lewton's weakest film, it has a superb "Lewton Walk." (Curiously, The Body Snatcher seems to be without a "Lewton walk," unless one counts the death of the ballad singer.) Indeed, other filmmakers recognized the power of the "Lewton walk" and began copying it. The Spiral Staircase (1946) even has a parody "walk," with the drunken housekeeper walking through the dark, before climaxing with an utterly serious "walk" taken by the heroine. Jacques Tourneur deployed what he learned from Lewton in 1958's Curse of the Demon, and the non-horror, neo-noir Cape Fear (1962) gives its heroine a "Lewton walk" in her own home. The most recent use of the "walk" happens in the new Hammer Studio's The Woman in Black (2012).

A third delight in Lewton's films is Elizabeth Russell an actress with unforgettable moments in several of Lewton's films. A striking blonde, but not with conventional "movie star" looks,

Russell makes an unforgettable appearance in Cat People as the strange woman in the Serbian restaurant who walks up to the wedding party and says "Moya sestra?" to Irena, reminding her that she will never be rid of the "old country's" claim on her despite her marriage to an American. It is a brief scene but central to the film's theme. and it drives home to the viewer that Irena's fate is inescapable.

Russell also had a small, but memorable role in The Seventh Victim, as Mimi, neighbor to Jacqueline, the heroine. Mimi confesses to Jacqueline, who is being stalked by a Satanic cult, that she has a fatal illness and is afraid of dying. In the film's last scene, Mimi tells Jacqueline that she is going out to have a night on the town despite knowing it will kill her. Jacqueline goes into her apartment and ends her persecution by hanging herself. As Mimi walks down the stairs, we hear Jacqueline's chair hit the floor, and we know both women will soon be dead.

However, Russell's most important role is in Curse of the Cat People as Barbara, a truly disturbing character. The adult daughter of the eccentric old actress who dotes on Amy, the child heroine of the movie, Barbara hates Amy for stealing her mother's love. At the film's climax, Barbara confronts the child, and the viewer is frightened that she will attack the child. Russell is so intense in this scene that the viewer is as upset watching this confrontation as watching the Frankenstein Monster accidentally drowns Maria.

Speaking of the Frankenstein Monster, there is a moment in Curse of the Cat People when Amy, after an argument with her father, runs through a snowstorm looking for her imaginary friend. As she runs, she yells "My friend! My friend!" The moment suggests the scene in Bride of Frankenstein when the Monster is driven out of the old hermit's house by hunters and runs through the woods shouting "Friend! Friend!" The echo of Monster as lonely child and lonely child as monster isn't forced. Perhaps most viewers don't pick up on it, but this is a moment which suggests that Lewton was not only an enemy of the Universal horror films but was able to pay tribute to them.

Curse of the Cat People itself is a lovely film and a true sequel to Cat People in that the subject of both films is loneliness and not lycanthropy. The sequel leaves it unclear if the "friend" played by Simone Simon is just a figment of the imagination conjured up by Amy's loneliness or if is the "actual" ghost of Irena from Cat People. What is beyond doubt is the skillful picture of a bright child shunned by the other children, in part through her own mistakes, and misunderstood by her parents. Lewton apparently incorporated some things from his childhood into this film, and the resulting emotional realism is powerful.

After Lewton made Curse of the Cat People, RKO let him make non-horror movies, only to go back on their word when box office receipts dipped. To make sure Lewton made horror movies, RKO brought Boris Karloff over to be Lewton's star.

This provoked some big changes for Lewton, who was not happy to work in the horror genre again and who was not keen on working with Karloff. Lewton's early films, from 1942's Cat People to 1944's Curse of the Cat People, had been set in the present with female protagonists. Lewton did not think Karloff would be believable in a contemporary American setting, and so his last three movies were set in the past. While Lewton and Karloff quickly became friends, a number of critics regard Lewton's Karloff films as a step down.

As I said earlier, Isle of the Dead does not work for me. Filming on this movie began before The Body Snatcher, only to be suspended when Karloff hurt his back. When Karloff recovered, The Body Snatcher was filmed, and when work resumed on Isle of the Dead, the script had been rewritten and a major female character removed. (Joel E. Siegel in <u>Lewton: The Reality of Terror</u> has a too brief discussion of this.)   Given this troubled origin, it is perhaps not surprising that <u>Isle of the Dead</u> stands at or near the bottom of my list of Lewton films.

However, <u>The Body Snatcher</u> and <u>Bedlam</u> gave Karloff two of his best performances, as Cabman Gray and Master Sims. While Karloff's Frankenstein Monster showed us the humanity in an inhuman creature, Gray and Sims are all too human monsters of cruelty.

Based on a story by Robert Lewis Stevenson, <u>The Body Snatcher</u> is, perhaps, Lewton's best film. There are no awkward moments, such as the scene in <u>Cat People</u> when the panther corners Oliver and Alice at the office and then retreats when Oliver's engineering tool sort of looks like a cross. Instead, everything in <u>The Body Snatcher</u> fits together like a finely crafted watch, ticking toward a shattering climax. Nothing overtly scary happens in the film's first ten minutes, but all the plot points that will drive the characters to their doom are introduced, and then the tension begins to build without relenting.

Compared to the other films, <u>The Body Snatcher</u> has the best cast of any Lewton film. Yes, Bela Lugosi seems lethargic if not ill as the doomed servant, but the film survives this misfortune. Russell Wade is superb as the idealistic medical student who is the film's hero. Wade projects an appealing personality, strong and intelligent and greatly outshines the "heroes" in Lewton's contemporary films. Meanwhile, Henry Daniell is brilliant as the arrogant, and tragic, Dr. MacFarlane. The true protagonist of <u>The Body Snatcher</u>, convinced of his own genius and rightness, MacFarlane is one of the most interesting horror movie protagonists.

Yet as good as the cast is, Boris Karloff manages to own the movie. Cabman Gray appears first as a charming, grandfatherly chap, paying attention to a crippled little girl. Later, a sly, cruel side of his personality shows through as he deals with an intimidated medical student. Ultimately, we see Gray as a cruel tyrant, exulting in his power over MacFarlane, the possibility he has of ruining this man's life. However, even as we see Gray's cruelty, Karloff (and Lewton) lets us see that he is cruel because his own dreams have been thwarted and crushed by the system that supports men like MacFarlane. When Gray's cruelty explodes in some of the most violent action in any Forties horror film, it seems as natural as breathing. Even though he is killed by MacFarlane, the viewer is not surprised when Gray's hatred seems to reach from beyond the grave to drag the arrogant doctor down with him.

Bedlam is not as assured a film as The Body Snatcher. It lacks the powerful structure of the earlier film, and it seems more of an attempted horror movie-historical film hybrid than a single-minded horror film. (Lewton intended that his next movie with Karloff would be about the career of Blackbeard the pirate, which suggests a move away from horror.) Also, one suspects that Bedlam, like Isle of the Dead and The Ghost Ship, was intended as an anti-fascist drama. All three movies are about petty tyrants who bring doom upon themselves. In Isle of the Dead and Bedlam, Karloff's characters are exposed as weak men who are quickly struck down and overthrown. Revealing the menace was just a "paper tiger" ripe for overthrow doesn't make for a first-rate horror movie.

However, Karloff gives a first-rate performance in Bedlam. Master Sims is a horror movie villain with a keen appreciation of social status. He always knows where he stands in relation to other people, and he acts accordingly. Consequently, he takes a lot of humiliation in Bedlam, being kept waiting in an aristocrat's parlor while the aristocrat's black houseboy comes and goes. (And Karloff's face shows that this truly grinds on Sims.) The aristocrat's mistress strikes him in the face with a riding quirt, and Sims takes it.

When he tries to interest the aristocrat in his cousin (Elizabeth Russell) as a replacement, his cousin's lower-class diction makes Sims squirm in embarrassment.

There are scary moments in <u>Bedlam</u>, such as when the Quaker hero comes to visit the heroine in the asylum and must walk down a darkened hallway, past the grasping hands of the lunatics. However, the main thrust of the movie is that reason shall triumph over ignorance and tyranny. Sims' rule over Bedlam is overturned, the heroine is restored to society, and one leaves the movie with an "upward and onward" sense that mankind's worst days are behind it.

<u>Bedlam</u>, however, has never enjoyed the popularity of <u>Cat People</u> and <u>The Body Snatcher</u>, films in which darkness wins or extracts a high cost in defeat. It is this grimness, a non-Hollywood realization that happy endings aren't in the cards, that perhaps gives Val Lewton's films their pull on those who watch them obsessively. Decades later, the loneliness of Irena and the bitterness of Cabman Gray can be recognized and identified with by those who would rather watch old horror movies than Judy Garland-Mickey Rooney movies in which a bunch of spirited kids put on a musical in a barn.

Ultimately, Val Lewton wasn't a winner in the Hollywood game. RKO shut down his unit after <u>Bedlam</u>, promising him the chance of producing bigger movies. It never panned out, and Lewton moved from studio to studio before dying in early middle age. He was gone, but his films continued to exert a pull, whether watched in film societies and college classrooms, or thanks to the late, late show and then VHS and DVD. Even now, in the age of streaming, Lewton's dark vision continues to fascinate.

To paraphrase the dying words of Cabman Gray, we shall never be rid of him.

"Moya Sestra"

The uninvited guest at the wedding feast
      sinister and catlike
reveals to all that the handsome American
wed the wrong woman
and a funeral shall follow.

Irena starts with terror at her greeting
      "My sister"
in the forgotten tongue of the
curse-laden Old Country,
a reminder of inescapable fate
and unchangeable essence.

She is my sister too
      this mysterious woman
who greets me in my American life
and calls out to the loneliness
and darkness of my inner self.

Never be rid of me, she might
      well say
as I write another horror story
or think about another horror movie
while the merry parade goes past.

Acknowledgements

"Zombies Walk Among Us" and "A Ticket to the Night Zoo" were written in the Nineties, as was an early version of "My Sister." I wrote "Shadows and Torment" in 2000 for the Odyssey Fantasy Writers Workshop and "The Man Who Knew Karloff" in 2001 for The Never-Ending Odyssey (TNEO). In the mid-2000s, I rewrote "My Sister" and expanded it by a third, while "His Queen of Darkness" was written in the late 2000s.

"My Sister" got Honorable Mention Fiction in the Wytheville Chautauqua Creative Writing Contest in 2008. "His Queen of Darkness" won First Place Fiction in the Wytheville Chautauqua Creative Writing Contest in 2009. "Moya Sestra" won Second Place Poetry in the Wytheville Creative Writing Contest in 2011.

I'd like to thank my Odyssey classmate Laura Whitton for her kind words about "Zombies Walk Among Us" and "A Ticket to the Night Zoo" and Dora Goss for her enjoyment of "Shadows and Torment." Barbara Campbell's comments on "His Queen of Darkness" helped me strengthen that story, and I will always appreciate her enthusiasm for "The Man Who Knew Karloff" at the 2001 TNEO. I also appreciate Jeanne Cavelos' kind words about "Karloff."

"Shadows and Torment" was enormously improved by the suggestions of the late Charles L. Grant, who enjoyed the Val Lewton references scattered throughout. He was a kind and gracious man, and I am always glad that he read this story.

Thanks also to Jennifer Mullins, James Ryan and Wendy Welch of the Big Stone Gap Writers Group. They read and commented on "My Sister" and "His Queen of Darkness."

That was the acknowledgement section for the first edition of this book.

Despite the passing of years, Val Lewton has continued to keep his grip on my imagination, and for the second edition of <u>His Queen of Darkness</u>, I have added four stories from <u>The Dream Cabinet of Dr. Kino</u> ("The Tears of Midnight," "Heart of Dark Cypress," "Dread," and "Cursed"), one from <u>Lost Shadows</u> ("Lady of the Beasts") and one from <u>Shadows of Forgotten Ancestors</u> ("Night Falls on the Marloveks.") I have also included "Never Be Rid of Him: Thoughts on Val Lewton," an essay from <u>The Horrible Possible and the Horrible Impossible</u>.

I have no doubt that I will still find Lewton and his films influencing me as I continue to write. Perhaps a third edition of <u>His Queen of Darkness</u> shall be necessary someday.

As always, thanks to my wife Elizabeth and my daughter Olivia and son Ethan Samerdyke for their patience and forbearance with me as I wrote.

Sheldon Wigod was the manager of the New Mayfield Repertory Cinema in Cleveland in the late Seventies and the early Eighties. The wallpaper in the NMRC was faded and peeling in spots, and cobwebs clung to the chandeliers, but, frankly, that made the New Mayfield the best spot for discovering the sorcery of <u>Cat People</u> and <u>I Walked With a Zombie</u>, a double feature that sparked an intense discussion among perfect strangers one fondly remembered night.

Although the New Mayfield closed at the end of 1985, in some ways this book is the continuation of that evening's discussion of the magic and power of Val Lewton.

Made in the USA
Columbia, SC
10 March 2022